Retail Commando

━━━━━━━━━━━━━━ ◆ ━━━━━━━━━━━━━━

Retail Commando

◆

essays, stories + other near misses

James Stegall

Writers Club Press
San Jose New York Lincoln Shanghai

Retail Commando
essays, stories + other near misses

All Rights Reserved © 2000 by James Stegall

No part of this book may be reproduced or transmitted in any form or by any means, graphic, electronic, or mechanical, including photocopying, recording, taping, or by any information storage retrieval system, without the permission in writing from the publisher.

Writers Club Press
an imprint of iUniverse.com, Inc.

For information address:
iUniverse.com, Inc.
5220 S 16th, Ste. 200
Lincoln, NE 68512
www.iuniverse.com

These stories are 100 percent fiction. Some of them project the names of "real" public figures onto made-up characters in made-up circumstances. Where the names of corporate, media, military, or political figures are used here, those names are meant only to denote figures, images, the stuff of collective dreams; they do not denote, or pretend to private information about, actual 3-D persons, living, dead, or otherwise.

Part of "Office Sex For Dummies" makes minor use of Michael Crichton's *Travel's* (Ballantine Books, 1988, pp. 101-2), for critical purposes.

Cover Photography by oops! design

ISBN: 0-595-15700-9

Printed in the United States of America

For Beth

Contents

Essays 1
    Retail Commando: a guide for responsible holiday consumption 3
    Cupid's Boxing Ring 15
    Getting Out Alive: a long strange trip through basic training 20
    A Modern Marriage Problem 32
    Office Sex for Dummies 35
    What the Marlboro Man Has To Say 39

Interviews 47
    Brian Michael Bendis is through being crime noir's best-kept secret 49
    Gender-Specific, New-Wave, Girl-Powered Punk Rock: The Third Sex ... 53
    Mike Allred: the skinny on comics' resident mad scientist 63

Stories 71
    We Have Rules 73
    The Wall Mirror 78
    The Springfield Girl 89
    Driving Under the Influence 106

Seventh Beer Thoughts *112*

Wild Duck: Eugene, Oregon *118*

Stereo *122*

At the Window *125*

Don't Wake *128*

Acknowledgements 149

Essays

Retail Commando:
a guide for responsible holiday consumption

I've rented a U-Haul: one of those *Maximum Overdrive* eighteen-wheelers they shouldn't make available to the general public. I could probably fit a Winnebago in the trailer.

That's good.

I've got a few items spread on the seat beside me: a bag of fudge-covered espresso beans, a jug of pink wine and—my favorite: brighter, spicier, more iridescent than a peacock's fan—fliers and catalogs of all colors and creed. I've got clothing stores, jewelry stores, computer warehouses, stationary supply houses, bridal boutiques, bookstores, music stores and supermarkets.

Oh yeah, they're like a cheesecake, and I worship cheesecake, right before you dive in: more creamy and savory in the imagination than any mortal experience could ever hope deliver—sweet, shiny invitations of endless love and caring, hungry for my attendance.

They love me, need me: *No Money Down! Ninety Days Same As Cash! Lowest Prices In Town! Get The Best Deal! Satisfaction Guaranteed!*

These are my Christmas cards, my tokens of good cheer. I've been a double-shift slave for the Man all year long for today—so I can meet them head on. I don't want to disappoint anybody. No, sir: I've got a big fat wad of filthy money smoldering a hole in my pocket. I'm here to please.

I grind gears and bound off.

It's 6:30 in the morning. I cover ten parking spots with the big ass of my U-Haul. That's okay. While the brakes hiss empty I choke down the espresso beans between swills of wine. Out of beans, I up-end the jug until it's all gone, wipe my mouth with a lusty, "Aah!"

I pat myself down as I join the line of eager folks waiting outside the mall doors, certain I have everything: air-horn, gum, pocket knife, handkerchief, cash, Mace, .45 automatic. I smile genially at the mom in front of me. I'm a good scout.

7 a.m. The rush (baby, RUSH!) begins.

Slowed down. Hearts pounding. And the doors open. Here's the frenzy—the seized, in-taken preparatory breaths of a thousand sale-maddened mothers ravenous for the golden buy, the magnificent kill: the trophy of their Child's Love. This is the race.

We're off. I surf them like a wave—they splash off the aisles, howling like wolves, hungry eyes snapping at the fat shelves, jostling, hustling. A million shopping cart wheels squeal and burn, clacking on the shiny tile like chomping teeth. Hear the deep, rabid breathing.

I'm with them: injected into the flow, caught up in the clot, rushed straight into the heart of America's life blood economic machine. This is the mainline. This is the bottom line. Right here is where shopper meets product and only the best goes home in the stylish twine-handled bags. Pure democracy. Here are the poor, the starving, the huddled masses, wide-eyed and hot for satisfaction, for the moment of gratification. This is great. This is beautiful. This is Capitalism and it gives me a shiny smile, like some fat Roman aristocrat smack in the middle of a writhing drunken orgy. I know what's good.

(Self-awareness is always the real bonus.)

Everybody's the same. They're at the top of their form, by God. They wait all year long for this. They dream about this. Sure it's for family, for the kids, for giving and love and time to share and the Salvation Army guy clanging his damn bell for nickels. Home For The Holidays. But I know better. I've seen backstage, glimpsed the mottled soul of this show. I've seen its backers, its slathering face: Conquest. This is "I've got it and you don't!" Survival of the fittest. Sure they know it's all a scam—how MTV, Saturday morning cartoons and Fruity Pebbles manipulate their kids, make them scream for specific rare prizes: Tickle Me Elmo, Finger Nail Fun, Buzz Lightyear, Fort Legoredo, Sea Monkeys—Oh, they know it and they could end it. But if it ended, where would they taste the thrill of the hunt, the mad chase, the heat of battle—combat, baby?

This is war. They love this. It's better than chocolate. Better than sex: it's glory—primal and vicious glory. It tastes good.

They know this. Dare you trespass in the proving ground of motherhood? Here in the Toy Department, behold the mighty clash of titans as they wage dire conflict throughout the cramped, dizzy aisles. They're bad! They'll punk you out. They'll bite your fingers off, rip you apart, swallow you whole and cackle. They move fast in those stretch pants and sweat shirts!

But not faster than Mace. It takes a couple direct face hits, some crying and choking, but they learn to leave me alone. Animals.

I feel sorry for the discount retail people: they're Mom-Land. Kmart, Wal-Mart, Target, Shopko—all writhing with hissing moms, petulant and ruthless. I can hear the tortured cries even now: "What do you *mean* you're sold out? When's the next truck? Can you order it? Well, who knows then? I want the manager!"

I leave Mom-Land and journey into Boutique-Land. Which means:

Welcome to the Great American Shopping Mall. But this isn't any mere strip mall. This is a Shopping Center. A multi-tiered temple of consumption. A fairy land of fantasy and joy, alive with cardboard sprites and jerky robotic elves. This is the land of fulfillment, where anything can be had for a price, and the populace sates its petty desires and ego trips on the slave-like employees. This is where America finds self-expression, satisfaction, meaning and entertainment.

But the mall is a cultural center as well. Behold: the Denizens of the Mall, those for which the mall has become the current version of a nineteenth century asylum—a place to dump those society would rather forget.

These are the mallrats: society's bastard children, run away to be raised by the shopping mall, the only authority they recognize. They hang out in crowds by the phones with their bleached heads, piercings and snide "Screw you for caring," attitudes.

Next, observe the homeless, sitting in the food court talking to themselves, nursing single cups of coffee all day long. See them in front of the movie store watching whatever selection is playing on the big screen by the door. Find them in the restrooms trying to conduct personal hygiene without removing any of their clothes or to get warm by holding their coats open to the hand drier. The mallrats shoot them with spit wads.

After the homeless come the retarded people. For these endlessly happy, optimistic individuals the mall is a playground. There are toys to play with, shopping carts to push, displays to ride, employees to hound. They frolic like kittens and puppies. They play the Nintendo display for hours, or grab carts and "shop" for items all over a store—only to ditch the cart so an employee can return everything.

Then you see the wheelchair-bound, victims of debilitating diseases whose families abandon them to make circuits of the mall all day in their electric wheelchairs or read romance novels in sunlit corners. (On what criteria do they choose their reading?)

Visiting in their domain is you: the cow-like consumer, not knowing what you want but experiencing a lemming-like compulsion to migrate to the mall and graze until some form of satisfaction is found through consumption.

You've got to look good, smell good, slice, dice and julienne. You must turn your labor into possession or life holds no gratification. Where is the meaning? At J.C. Penny, my friend. Ties are the meaning of life. No tie is like another so you can buy them forever.

You think I'm wrong?

Time to get busy.

I begin my spending frenzy like a Bulimic passing into a binge/purge haze. I need small purchases to lubricate my pockets, get some change. I need to try on one shirt, like it, and buy every color available. I'm Jay Gatsby for a day, baby.

I hit the boutique shops so I can wow the sales girls while my bills are still big. I want them to ask how I'm doing while I'm trying on all the latest styles: plastic, rave, phat, leather, latex…I want them to hand me clothes and give me their opinions. I want them to be my mother, my girlfriend. They tell me how great I look even when I look like an idiot.

I love going into those athletic shoe stores and just buying the most expensive shoe there, just to rub it in the face of the cocky salesman lacing up my moon shoe Nikes. He's not so hot. Not when he sees the brand names on the bags I'm carrying!

Oh yeah, I'm feeling it now.

Next I hit the electronics stores, nodding intently while sweaty salesmen rap on home theater, Smart TV, stereo components and why I should buy their crappy Tandy computers. I buy one anyway, just because I can. Then I go crazy with a remote control car, racing it over the toes of some fat guy outside the doors. (Mace quiets his complaints.) I get the car too.

I hit the gift shop and snarf up plastic doggie crap, a Christmas card with a picture of baby Jesus and the word "fart" inside and a sweaty hunk poster for my mom.

I reel out, stumbling beneath the massive weight of my buying power and beat feet out to the U-Haul. On the way, a girl eyes the size of my load and approves of me with a smile.

I love Christmas.

Me: "What I'm talking about here is *disassociation*. Oh yeah, this is free association, the free marketplace of ideas. I'm talking about chopping the world off like a bad toe and watching the worms from afar. Then you swoop down from the outside with a war cry and dream and scatter those maggots, just send them *screaming*. That's the world. That's how you've got to look at it. Conquest is the point. Conan had it down, baby."

Cashier: "Really? Paper or plastic?"

That's why I love cashiers. Cashiers just listen to you and smile. Then they take your money and wish you a nice day. I love that plastic Fifties paradigm flashing with smiles, waves and "Howya doin' neighbor?" It's so damn happy that I go shopping just for the cashiers.

Once I was in line behind this bastard who started harassing the cashier. "God, but you're ugly," he said to her. "Why do they always hire such ugly people here?" he asked. "Why are you all so ugly?"

Maybe all cashiers aren't runway models but they're nice and you have to respect them. I just grabbed that bastard by his soft throat and ground his face into the counter until he apologized. I wiped his face all over his own drool, squeezing his love handles and whispering in his ear: "Squeal like a piggy—*squeal!*"

I have to admit I enjoyed myself and was quite pleased by the cashier's satisfied wink—and I wasn't any less vindicated when Shopko asked me to leave their store.

My turning point came two years ago in a Fred Meyer store. It was down to the wire and the mob was crazed, grabbing up anything it could get its hands on—picture frames, rolls of fabric, K-Tel compilations—that might function as a gift. I had finally finished my gift buying and was ready to get out, when I witnessed an event that would change my life forever.

I watched an old man walk up to a red vested employee and demand: "Christmas wrap!"

The employee paused. "Excuse me?" he asked.

"Christmas wrap!" the old man repeated.

"You're looking for Christmas wrap?" the employee rephrased.

This employee was a man on the edge, obviously. Who wouldn't be? The poor guy couldn't walk five feet without getting grabbed, poked, snapped, whistled or yelled at. Everyone referred to him as, "Hey, Fred Meyer Guy!"

The old man stared at him, seemingly dumbfounded as to why he couldn't abuse and then be handed his prize like everyone else.

The employee shook his head sadly.

"Look at me," the Fred Meyer Guy ordered. A quality in his voice sent a shrill vibe through the mob. As though the aisle were a playground, a circle immediately cleared.

"What's wrong with you?" the employee demanded. "Am I so worthless I don't even deserve complete sentences? Or are you just too stupid to talk to me like a human being?"

The old man tried to reply but the employee stopped him. "No," he continued, addressing the mob now. "You have to snap at me, yell at me, squeal at me like hogs! Why don't you open your stupid eyes and look for the Christmas wrap, you cows? Look at you! My God, I've been at this job for three years and I still get treated like dirt by you people—just because you're all little brats who can't get their own Christmas wrap. All of you! Sniveling children!

He shook his head. "How would you like it if I came into your places of work, ripped your files apart, hounded you with questions, moved your belongings, belittled you, grabbed at you and barked commands at you for nine hours a day?"

The employee mimed tearing through files with chopping motions of his arms.

He shook his head, declaring: "I'm not going to tell you what to buy your kids anymore. I'm not going to tell you what you need to be happy. I'm not going to give you what the TV tells you to want. Not if you don't have the common decency to talk to me like adults instead of a bunch of caveman hunter-gatherers slobbering for raw fish. Animals!"

He laughed desperately. "Christmas wrap!" His head moved side to side and his voice grew child-high. "How about 'Excuse me, could you tell me where the Christmas wrap is?' Followed by, 'Oh, thank you'"

He returned his gaze to the old man. "No, apparently you're incapable of that. Well, I refuse to serve your childish satisfaction like some kind of indentured slave to retail!

"I quit, asshole."

He ripped off his vest and stalked from the store.

People should have clapped. But they just looked around. Their hunter-gatherer instincts swallowed up whatever significance his stand may have held.

In a moment the crowd trembled and returned to its roaring and rumbling through the aisles. The old man huffed indignantly and started asking the people around him where the Christmas wrap was. Nobody knew.

I stared after the ex-employee. I was impressed, anyway.

I feel successful and meaningful during the Holidays. I'm at a buffet of gratification and I can eat and eat and only get comfortably full. By clothing my consumption in the guise of "Gift Giving" I can rationalize my greed into charity. Oh, it feels so good to stroke my consumer impulses, flex my buying power.

That's right: I'm Godzilla. And the mall is my Tokyo.

Watch them scatter beneath me!

In this country you are meaningless and small unless you "own" lots and lots of things. I own everything. I've experienced human contact with more cashiers and sales people this morning than I have with my family all year.

Oh yeah, I'm hitting full stride now. In the past few minutes I've come to own a washer and drier set, a central heating unit and deluxe router. Look how big the boxes are! I feel pretty good because I beat an old lady to the heating unit (dazed her with the air horn, took her out with Mace). Hey, it was the last one at the clearance price.

The U-Haul is filling up. Slowly my Winnebago space has shrunk to Toyota space. Now it's full. I pull the rear door closed and turn around, resting my back against the cool steel. I mop my brow. It hasn't been a terrible day. When I ran out of Mace I had to use my pocket knife to chase off some geeked-out action figure collectors. It got a little hairy, but I got the Princess Leia. All's good. I straighten my clothes and head back in for lunch.

I have just enough money for a value meal. While I'm waiting in line a fat lady charges the counter and confronts the boy at the register with a slimy piece of beef dangling from her thumb and forefinger. An expression of terror and disgust rolls across the boy's face as she drops the patty in his open palm and demands a coupon for a free burger. Forget high school: these are the times that try teenage lives.

I dole out my final pennies and sit down with my burger and fries. My glow is fading. I may be dressed in fine new clothes and soon to be driving a U-Haul packed with crap, but I still don't feel good. Nobody wants to talk to me now. I stare forlornly around the food court at the happy people, families and couples, teenagers waiting for movies. I feel a vast emptiness. It's horrible to be faced by what you can't buy. Even the ugly, fat consumers wandering around in herds have each other. Me? I have nothing but that moment of transaction when I am one with the economy and the world recognizes my contribution—and the sales girl smiles and thanks me. Then I'm booted through the door until I can come back with more money. Work, steal, whatever.

We live in a world of whores.

Sure, that's it. Oh boy, I'm angry now. I toss my tray on the floor and jump to my feet. I've got energy but no purpose. Then I see them: the robotic elves. Leering at me and waving their stupid mannequin arms. All over, the mall is sparkling and flashing, a million reflections of holiday cheer, smiles and laughter. I can't take it.

What can I do when I have nothing else to do? How can I show them they can't step on me? How can I cope? How can I react?

Oh, but I know: Violence.

Smile.

I break through the food court, leaping tables, tossing bawling children. I've got places to go. I reach for my waistband and produce the .45, receive a gasp from a nearby housewife, now screams. Yeah, that sounds good.

Everybody's trying to get away from me, scrambling for somewhere to hide in the wide open store fronts. There's nowhere to go. Hide behind your shopping bags, you fools. Suck floor behind the plastic trees. I'm coming for you.

I spot my goal in the distance. They haven't seen me yet, and as I burst through the line of children, everyone stares at me in a weird silent awkwardness—until the screams split through and they understand, they know to be afraid of something. But I've already tossed them out of my way, scooped the now-sobbing toddler out of his lap and taken him by the throat, shoved his lumpy body against the throne they've set him in. He's just a bum. He's just a big liar.

I put the .45 to Santa's head.

This is the sort of moment most people dream about but could never figure out how to live through. They're all watching me. In the distance I hear Mall Cops shouting. Muzak is still chiming through the loudspeakers.

But the mall itself is silent. It's an unfamiliar, ugly sound. It's like static. I have to say something, though. I've come this far.

I rest the pistol's muzzle against the old man's temple and study him for a beat. He's a pretty good likeness, but alcohol has burst the blood vessels on his cheeks. I suppose it's not enough that Santa should be fake, but of course he's an alcoholic as well. Welcome to the Millennium. I feel his throat throb as he attempts to swallow through my clenched hand.

"Tell me something, guy," I say. I have to say something. I loosen my grip so he can speak. "Tell me: Are you Santa Claus? Is there such a person as Santa Claus? Or are you just an alcoholic liar?"

I watch the confusion march across his eyes. "What?" he gasps.

"I asked you to tell the kiddies here if there is such a person as Santa Claus," I command, grinding the muzzle into his rubbery temple. "Go on, now. Tell them the truth."

I force him to his feet, facing the trembling toddlers and parents.

"Tell them the truth now, Santa," I repeat.

"I—" He pauses. It takes a draw-back *click* of the pistol's hammer to convince him to finish. "No, there is no Santa Claus," he says. He bows his head. "I'm sorry."

Jesus, he's crying.

"See," I shout, laughing. "See! He's a fraud. This is all a scam for your money! Don't you see? Christmas is a scam, you fools!"

Nobody says anything. No applause. Of course.

Somewhere a kid starts bawling as well. I can also hear a Mall Cop shouting into his walkie-talkie: "I'm telling you I've got a *situation* here!"

I think my moment's ended.

Scratch this. I yank Santa off the stage and drag him through the circle of onlookers, past the trembling security guards and through the front doors. Police sirens threaten in the distance. I hang on to the old man long enough to get the U-Haul warmed up. He doesn't say much.

At least he's stopped sniveling. In a minute I toss him out of the cab, then fling a toaster after him—for his trouble. I don't need it.

I roar out of the parking lot, smashing through some cops, racing for half an hour while I get away. I had planned on heading for Montana and Freeman territory. But I don't think I'd like it there. Too many antelope and not enough Seven-Elevens. Besides, just like the rest of our dysfunctional nation, my massive consumption binge is only half the picture. Come December 26th I'll have to purge myself and return all this crap.

I'd forgotten about that—how good it feels to empty myself of all these heavy belongings. I'll be sure and lose all my receipts. That way they'll give me in-store credits and I'll have to buy all new stuff. I'll get to talk with the return girl. Maybe even argue with her. Yeah.

Oh, yeah. That sounds pretty good.

Cupid's Boxing Ring

So my lady and I are in a fight and I'm begging a fourth-story window to let me up.

Freezing rain bangs my head like bullets while the women on the first, second and third floors all laugh at me. They've been here, or they wish their man would grovel like I am groveling now. Public humiliation is one of the keys to my girl's lock. She likes to make me shout "I love you," in restaurants and shopping malls. When I satisfy her she gets this smug "Damn, right" expression that's sort of my reward but more a warning to onlooking women. I figure it's a pheromone thing.

Eventually she'll let me in. Then I'll get hit by that angry face of hers, hard as a glass ashtray. We never yell at each other at first. We accuse silently for hours. We edge problems in half-conversation until she gets disgusted and confronts me. Then she lets it fly.

Harsh words are her flair. She lobs one-liners at me like a Nazi grenadier. She dredges up pillow-talk from nine months ago and holds me accountable. She swings questions like emotional wrecking-balls at the core of my devotion. Then she enjoys the havoc.

I was raised the silent, denying sort and I'm no good against her honesty. She knows that, so she isn't as cruel as she can be, but she can't help it sometimes. Just like I can't help locking anger behind the doors in my head. Until she probes her finger around just a little too hard and the doors burst open, and it's on.

So we rage back and forth until we get sweaty and tired like little kids and finally collapse in each other's arms, sniffling.

That's the moment I'm healed. Emptied of the pent anger and resentment, with nothing inside but the sensation of holding her, consumed by the reaffirmation of love, I'm actually thankful that we fought. That moment, sweeter than the first warm instant of love, is what I now live for. I exist to be cracked open so she can burrow into my soul like I was some kind of rotten apple. And I am rotten. I'm sick and I hate life just like every other sorry kid out there and loving her is my only redemption. She expurgates my guilt, soothes my pain, eases my solitude in this world. Without her I have nothing. She is the beauty and the reason in my life.

Transformed by the fire of passion.

I'm addicted to it. Whether it's good or bad, if we're star-crossed to have these ups and downs, or whatever else—I don't care. Of the many things I love about being with her, this is paramount: She gives me passion. Well, I can't say she gives it to me, but it's something we create through the crackling combination of us. Powerful chemistry.

We're not crazy, and I know we're not unique. This white-water of ecstasy is well-known and often concealed. In any relationship there'll be highs and lows; anyone who says they and their partner have an easy time of it, that they never fight…I'm suspicious of them.

And a little sorry.

How can you know how brilliant life is unless you've tasted the pain, the misery, the soul-hurt of those basement lows? Ears ringing? The world wobbly through tears? The high of pure emotion? The knowledge of that point beyond all self-surrender? This is Orpheus and Eurydice love, Van Gogh love, love like in David Lynch films, love that infuriates and inspires, tattoo love. And when the two of you hit that hell-low point—here's the secret—there's nowhere to go but up. Like Seinfeld says: Now you've got makeup sex to look forward to.

I'm not advocating abuse and I'm not calling it a healthy cycle if it includes physical or emotional damage.

But here are the facts: People are real. The Leave It To Beaver fantasy leaves way too much out—interesting stuff, vivid stuff, stuff worth taking a good look at. We get irritated, we get angry. We get pissed off when someone puts their CDs in the rack wrong. That's life. Complacency is cruising along denying all these feelings, letting someone run your life by default simply because you never say so. Because you don't want to upset anybody or hurt anybody's feelings. Real life is communication and making your feelings known. Equality is the flower of that honesty and to bake a truly tasty cake you're going to break some eggs.

Passion is going to rise up like a spark plug and ignite some internal relationship combustion, emotion flaring and flaming, making itself recognized. That's right, *feeling*. A short transcript of such an episode:

There it is—this is how I feel. And this is how you feel and goddamn it you piss me off.

<Shock.> Well, I never knew I pissed you off. I've never seen this side of you before.

Ha. How you like me now?

Suddenly life has a wider horizon than before. (The scenario is drastically simplified for the slower readers. Spice it up with some door slamming, phone crashing, voice raising and tears.) All of a sudden the kernel of something true appears, a tiny drop much like love juice that two people heave and jerk for hours to create:

Honesty.

What else is there? What else is worth it?

There's a reason Socrates wanted those with eros banned from the perfect republic—they had the passion, the will, the integrity to accept no less. Open your eyes and see; blink and look again. There it is: reality. You just screamed and yelled and pulled down the walls and cried off the makeup and there you are, two people—in honest light.

Or as close an approximation as two people can make. Betwixt them's all that matters anyway. The alternative is a life much like the generic food aisle—until twenty-five years pass and one or the other of you wakes up and leaves. And then the opportunity you had, together, to mean something real to each other and to those around you, giving off these psychedelic waves of heat-honesty infecting more and more people, is forever, irrevocably lost. Sigh.

So the fight. The fight is like sex. But mental. The fight is the process and sometimes "fight" is too strong or too weak a term for what transpires. I like to think of it as the expression of self, the honesty that says I am me and you are you and right now we're not fitting. It's time to grind some gears and get the car rolling again.

Like Hellraiser says, "Delicious pain" can be just as revealing as that initial masking bliss. Passion is two sides of the same coin. Take a look at the edge of that coin to judge how close those attached emotions are—hence the intensity of makeup sex. An example of the wonderful, never boring, complexity inherent in every one of us.

We are all capable of making our desires known. There are whole bookstore sections devoted to the easiest ways to do that—they all amount to stylized combat, a martial arts of argument.

You'll need personality. You'll need a strong desire to make your needs known. A great vocabulary helps. Perfect memory is key. You'll also need big ears to catch all those counters your partner sends in retaliation. You'll need a big heart to absorb those explosions of emotion that might radiate Atom Bomb-like, and you'll need a thick skin to let the important through and to slough off the petty.

And it'll get petty. Kung Fu argument is best left to retirees who are, at their age, communicating during fights like people in their twenties. The people in their twenties and thirties hit auto-pilot to toddler and kindergartner levels of expression during times of emotional duress.

Uh-uh! Did too! Did not! I hate you! I hate you!

(Thank passion to keep even the seniors crackling like rice crispies.)

There's the mess. Jump in and untangle the snarl. And remember, if you didn't care, you wouldn't bother.

Staring up at the malevolent yellow light of her window through heavy needles of rain, I can't immediately explain why I am standing here. It might be a need for the last word. I could think she looks good naked. Maybe because I don't want to lose her, and this could be one of those important fights, whose real purpose and motivation aren't yet revealed to me.

It could be that right now I feel more alive than I ever have in my life, and this rollercoaster has been non-stop since the day we met. I couldn't ask for more.

So I should explain it's not the arguing I'm addicted to, it's the process of honesty—and its gateway to real life, this kaleidoscope, this magic carpet ride—because I was programmed in such a way that I can't give up truth about me or my feelings without a struggle. Life was plain oatmeal before her.

She's got her issues, too. But I don't know about all of them yet and I doubt I ever will. Life is long and we've only been together a year.

So the rain is coming down and women are laughing but I feel hot. In fact, I feel great. The ever-rising heat keeps the boredom away, keeps life close and real. And that's all right. Passion. Thank you.

Turn it up, baby.

Getting Out Alive:
a long strange trip through basic training

Welcome to Fort Leonard Wood, Missouri. It's December 10, 1993.

Tank playground and time-honored home of the United States Army's Engineers, Fort Leonard Wood is a lumpy square of rolling hills and jagged limestone valleys located in the northern section of Missouri. This time of year the hills are soft with a thick blanket of fallen oak leaves. Everywhere the black, naked trees reach like claws for the sky.

The weather races here: clouds roil and mutate in minutes, sweep across the ice-blue sky and disappear, or pile up and rage for half an hour, dumping hail, sleet, rain or snow. In the mornings air streams split the sky into separate camps of clouds, angry and serene.

You are eighteen years-old when you arrive in Missouri. This will be your first Christmas away from home. And you've chosen the worst time of year to visit Fort Leonard Wood.

Before you leave, a quarter of your platoon will suffer frost bite. You will learn to kill a man from 300 meters with absolute accuracy. You will throw live grenades. You will crawl in the mud like a worm. You will wait for three hours outside a psychiatrist's office, guarding a young man who nearly strangled himself with his boot laces. You will spend eight weeks with sixty men who hate each other. You will experience fear, loneliness, anger, hatred, confidence, accomplishment and triumph like you never have in your life.

You're in Basic Training.

You don't arrive in Basic right away. The first place they send you is called Reception Station. This is where you will have your head shaved—don't do it before-hand, they'll only make you do it again—get vaccinated, fitted with uniforms, issued an identification card, set up your Direct Deposit (you'll need the form from your bank; it may seem like a hassle but do it—direct deposit will save you waiting in endless lines for your paycheck), fill out a form for Soldier's Group Life Insurance ($200,000 for $16 a month) and have the picture taken that you mail home to Mom and Dad. Plus, they give you what they call "Casual Pay," which is an advance on your paycheck, and make you buy shower shoes, a shoe shine kit and other seemingly useless items. You don't have an address while at Reception Station, so for two weeks you receive no mail and feel lonely. But they do allow you a five minute phone call home.

You don't yet have Drill Sergeants. You have what are called TAC Sergeants. They never explain what "TAC" stands for. But these sergeants yell a lot and as punishment for talking or falling asleep make you stand outside in the cold for hours. You learn that Basic Training runs in cycles, and you will have to wait for your cycle to start. So in the dead time they march you around the base to rake leaves. You spend four days doing this.

Everyday the rumors mount about Basic's difficulty and Drill Sergeant cruelty as you watch those who came ahead of you ship out and new people arrive in civilian clothes. Already civilians look awkward to you.

You are also given a "Smart Book." This is a fat little book filled with "Tasks" and "Standards"—hundreds of tests—explaining how to perform every common skill expected of an infantry soldier. This is your Bible. Whenever you're not doing something else, you must read it.

You are also ordered to learn the three General Orders: 1. *I will guard everything within the limits of my post and quit my post only when properly relieved. 2. I will obey my special orders and perform all my duties in a military manner. 3. I will report violations of my special orders, emergencies, and anything not covered in my instructions to the Commander of the Relief.*

These, they tell you, are all you really need to know to be a successful, happy private.

Finally, the Tuesday you are to leave for Basic Training arrives and the TAC Sergeants march everyone to some long low buildings you have never seen before. In these buildings you are issued your dog tags. Then you sit down and wait. You realize the Army has a lot of waiting. "Hurry up and wait," everyone calls it. After three hours pass, two semi-trucks pull up outside and through the windows you watch three men jump from their cabs. These men are wearing the infamous "brown round" Drill Sergeant hats you remember from *Full Metal Jacket.* They don't look pleased.

A wave of fear and tension electrifies the room as everyone realizes what's happening and jumps to their feet, attempting to stand at attention. The doors burst open and the yelling begins.

If you want to make money during Basic Training you need two things: a Polaroid camera with lots of film, and electric hair clippers. However, these items are considered contraband and unless you hide them, they will be taken away and you'll do push ups. Hide them in your second pair of boots. Don't try to hide them in your civilian bag—that gets locked up for eight weeks. (But near the fourth week when you're allowed free time, try to persuade the Drill Sergeant to let you into your bag to "get your basketball shoes, so you can play basketball at the gym." This is a good time to get all the stuff you want.) You may have to get creative with the camera, due to its size. But, at two to three dollars a picture and four dollars a haircut, the risk is well worth the reward. Everyone wants pictures to send home, and haircuts at the Post Exchange are six dollars.

The first event in Basic Training is a shake down. The Drill Sergeants put you in formation in front of the barracks and make you empty all your belongings onto the ground in front of you. They then take liberty with your stuff—poking through your socks, looking through your wallet (commenting rudely on your girlfriend's picture) and making you hold up items whose names they call out, to ensure that you haven't lost anything between here and Reception Station. If you have any Aspirin, Tylenol or other painkillers or medicine, they will yell "Contraband!" and demand how they should know that these pills aren't crack, cocaine or smack. They then dump the pills out and step on them. If you have a prescription, let them know in a hurry—or else your medication could end up crushed. They also check running shoes. Anything but straight-forward running shoes will be considered wrong and you will have to buy new ones. Everything they consider contraband—radios, magazines, books, candy, Gameboys, etc.—goes into your civilian bag and gets locked up.

Then you are lined up alphabetically and marched into the barracks, where you are issued a bunk and a locker, and introduced to your "Battle Buddy"—the private who must either be with you or know where you are at all times. You are shown how to make your bunk and how to arrange your locker to standard, then given an hour to make it happen before your first inspection. Anyone who screws up along the way does many push ups.

Now you learn a new word: Standard. The Standard is the heart of Uniformity. Inspections are the method by which the Army upholds its Standard. So you get inspected a lot. Everything you do from this point on will be to the Army Standard, whether it is Physical Training or scraping wax off the floors with a razor blade. You also learn that the Drill Sergeant is the embodiment of the Army Standard. It is the Drill Sergeant's job to teach you the Standard way in which to perform every Army task. Knowing this, it becomes fairly easy to understand the Drill Sergeant's frame of mind: "I'm right, private, and you are always wrong."

Here's what the Drill Sergeants make you say when you're doing push ups at their feet: "Sergeant, Private [insert your name here] requests permission to speak, Sergeant."

"Speak," says the Drill Sergeant.

"Sergeant, thank you for conditioning my mind and body. Please feel free to do so at any time. Sergeant, Private Dork requests permission to recover!"

"Recover, private," yawns the Drill Sergeant.

This also demonstrates what graduates of Fort Leonard Wood Basic Training affectionately refer to as the "Sergeant Sandwich." When addressing a Drill Sergeant, you must begin and end your sentence with "Sergeant." This only happens at Fort Leonard Wood; tradition has it that in the past a conflict arose between the Drill Sergeants and the post commander, some General, and that was his order: That they should never be called "Drill Sergeant" by the trainees again. This doesn't make the Drill Sergeants happy. Ask them about it and you'll do pushups.

Time passes. You write to lots of people back home and find that few respond. But the letters keep you sane, stand as proof that you really did have another life somewhere else. Slowly your platoon finds itself reduced to complete unconscious uniformity. You begin talking with the same military expressions, the same generic Southern accent, walking left foot first, and humming marching cadence as though it were top forty.

During a typical day, you wake at 3:30 a.m. and have an hour to make your bed and clean the barracks. The Drill Sergeants, who arrive at 4:30, never like the platoon's job—so for the hour of physical training (PT) they line you up in the barracks hallways and make you jump between pushups, flutter kicks and running in place every time a whistle blows. Sometimes there are agonizing long periods between blasts; sometimes it comes so fast all you do is fall on your stomach, roll over and jump up again. This is called "Front, Back, Go."

During PT the Drill Sergeants disgustedly roam the halls, screaming at you, calling you weak, a pussy, loser, civilian. Then they choose some unlucky slow private to exact special torture upon. He gets to suffer flutter kicks with a rifle across his ankles. Finally it ends, after they have ground into the platoon's skulls that you are positively the worst, weakest, most undisciplined platoon they have ever, ever had.

It occurs to you that what they just screamed is probably the hardest part of all this—the fact that no matter how hard you try, you can never do anything right.

After breakfast, you have four hours of classes. Don't fall asleep, or you get to go in the back of the room or outside with the Drill Sergeant and "elevate your heart rate." Next, you have lunch, two more classes, then dinner. One more class and bed/personal time. You usually get to bed around 10:00 p.m., unless you wind up with Fire Guard, which means you get to waste a half-hour's sleep waxing the floors. Sleep is the most treasured commodity you have.

In the fourth week you begin Basic Rifle Marksmanship. Among many other things, you've already learned how to march (and suffered for every cross-eyed idiot who couldn't keep in step), how to kill with a bayonet (What makes the green grass grow? Blood, blood, bright red blood!), how to crawl during combat, how to fold your clothes the Army way and what a Command Sergeant Major is. Now you spend days at different rifle ranges learning every aspect of the M16A2 rifle.

"These weapons are toys, privates," a Drill Sergeant yells at you.

"Just shoot in the same place every time and the rifle will put you on target." Then he gazes lovingly at the black contraption of plastic and steel in his hands. "You can kill all day long with this mother fucker, privates," he says. "All day long."

You become intimate with the most effective personal weapon history has yet known. You clean it, take it everywhere, sleep with it during bivouac, and do extensive pushups with it laid across your knuckles if you're unlucky enough to drop it. The clatter of a M16A2 hitting the ground is one of the most distinctive sounds you will ever hear. A Drill Sergeant commanding, "Drop with it, private," soon follows.

You also learn a new definition of the word "Smoking." One of the first things your Drill Sergeant does upon your arrival is ask the formation in a loud, humorous voice: "Who here is dying for a smoke?" Since no tobacco is allowed in Basic Training, as well as no sexual contact (basically, nothing pleasurable), sure enough, some withdrawal-suffering fool raises his hand and shouts, "Sergeant, I do, Sergeant!"

"Come on out here in front, then," the Drill Sergeant answers in a honey voice. "I got something for you."

The private drops in front of us, of course. When he can no longer perform pushups, he is made to do flutter kicks, then sit ups, more push ups, jumping jacks, bear crawls, neck lifts—even something called the "Dead Cockroach" where he just twitches violently for fifteen minutes. You learn this process is called "Getting Smoked."

When a private stops moving, the Drill Sergeant says dryly: "You ain't cooked yet, private. Roll over and push." On freezing Fort Leonard Wood mornings, when the entire platoon gets smoked, it's not uncommon to find a cloud of condensing perspiration hovering above your bent, straining backs.

Being a Drill Sergeant is one of the most difficult jobs in the Army—they're in the barracks after you go to bed and often before you get up, and most of them have families. So Smoking seems to be their only outlet for creativity and enjoyment. Exercises range from the "MC Hammer" to the "Electric Chair" to the "Bus Driver," each an innovative torture in itself. Toward the end, as you really get into shape, new exercises become a masochistic pleasure.

The only thing you need say to tap your Drill Sergeant's creative energy is: "Can't smoke a quitter, Sergeant!" This makes them feel their patriotic duty.

During one smoking, as you agonize through your fifteenth minute of situps, your Drill Sergeant leans close to your ear and whispers, "You know what, private? I love this shit. This shit makes my dick hard."

When you first arrived, the Drill Sergeants said you would never forget them. Now you know you'll have that sick bastard's voice in your head until you die.

Then you go through the gas chamber. They say it's for your benefit, so you will learn to trust the protective masks. You figure it's just one more torture to endure.

Supposedly the gas in the chamber contains nerve, choking and tear agents, so it is representative of the three kinds of gas experienced in combat. To put it in reference, they tell you it's 500 times stronger than Mace and 50 times stronger than riot gas. They say the gas will irritate your skin and make your mucous glands go crazy, so you'll salivate like a rabid dog and have spit and snot pouring out of your nose. Instant Pavlovian response. Don't touch your skin, they warn, after you go through, or it gets a lot worse. Loaded with this information, you are fed lunch and marched to the training area.

They line you up by platoon and start moving you through the little brick building by tens, like aliens in your green hoods and black rubber masks. As the door closes on the group ahead of you, you hear something go wrong inside. The Gas Master's voice rumbles unintelligibly over a loudspeaker. You hear him shouting. Someone is beating against the door and the guards grunt to hold it closed. Eventually the Gas

Master says something else and the opposite door bursts open. The ten spill out, masks off and choking, fanning their spread arms. Streamers of snot and saliva swing from their clenched faces.

The guards then open the door, revealing the smoky gas chamber, and scream for you to move. You are third in line. Nazi deathcamp images flood your mind. Your breathing is huge in your ears. You hear the door slam closed and clank as you are locked inside. While you were waiting, a Drill Sergeant came down the line checking the seal on each private's mask. He must not have done a very good job or some broke their seals because immediately the first private in line starts coughing and motioning at his mask. Turning, you see that another private has ripped his mask off and is doubled over, gagging. The room is hazy with smoke. It's strange to see the gas and not feel it. But you're breathing fine. You taste a little sulfur. Through a window in the facing wall your Drill Sergeants watch you and laugh. There is a red vertical line painted along the wall that you're not supposed to cross until told. The exit is beyond the line.

Okay, two of you are choking and reeling all over the chamber, begging the faces behind the window to let them out. No chance.

"Crack your masks," the loudspeaker shouts. "Show us your chins, privates!" You crack your mask and lift it above your chin, then wrench it back over your face, clear and reseal it. Again, you breathe fine.

"Take them off, privates!" says the speaker. "I want to see twenty eyeballs. Breathe, privates!" Without hesitation, you pull the protective mask off your head and breathe the gas.

Immediately your face starts to burn. The gas fills your lungs like insulation, like Styrofoam—it's thick, tastes like firework smoke, and completely immobilizes your lungs. You can't breathe. You take short, shallow little pin-prick breaths. Your eyes burn, suddenly so dry that it hurts to look anywhere but ahead. You stand gasping like a landed fish, flailing for release.

"All right," the loudspeaker says. "Get your right shoulder against the wall, privates."

Then the first private in line breaks for the door.

They warned you before that unless you did everything right they wouldn't let you out. Well, you aren't about to stay in there because of one dumb fuck who can't follow instructions. The second private in line is doubled over and unaware of everything—so you push him out of the way and grab the first private. Dragging him back, you shove him against the wall behind the line. Then you stand the private in front of you straight up against the wall. The door opens.

"Get out!" the loudspeaker commands. You stream out the door, arms wide, choking for cool air.

If you want to succeed in Basic Training you have to remain anonymous. You want your Drill Sergeant to stare at you half way through and demand, "Who the fuck are you?" (It can happen.) Don't have your girlfriend send you nude photographs (one private's girl sends him an old photo of her blowing him, which he proudly displays in his locker. This makes him immediately popular) or lingerie or anything else the Drill Sergeants might latch onto at mail call and turn into a torture device.

While the Drill Sergeants cannot deprive you of your mail, they can go through it if they choose, and declare anything they want contraband. Don't tell them you've been in college—they hate college students: (Oh, you got college, huh?)—or have a lot of money or brag about your sexual or physical prowess. They'll find ways to humiliate you.

Here's a cardinal rule: Don't lose anything. Losing even a glove means you have to tell the Drill Sergeants and they have to get you another one. This throws them into a rage. Plus, you have to pay for any lost items when you turn them all back in.

Also: Don't talk back. Don't get in fights. Do what you're told. Try and enjoy it.

They shock you awake. Ten of them exploding through the door, pinning your Battle Buddy, Johnson, to his bunk. But he's fighting back, screaming and biting. Ten privates can't hold him down. Still groggy, you find your watch and see that it's 1:30 a.m. Johnson throws someone against you. You push him off and watch as the mess of bodies surges in the tight space of the room, propelled by Johnson's rage. It quiets and you hear he's sobbing now. They've managed to cool him a little.

Suddenly Johnson screams and forces them off him. He smashes one private in the stomach and reaches for the door. They drag him back. This continues for nearly half an hour, until Johnson finally mellows to shallow crying. You've never seen anyone so crazy in all your life. Slowly the other privates leave the room, and you sit on the edge of his bunk to ask him what's wrong.

You want to laugh when he tells you that one of them made fun of his mother. You can understand a fight, but not this. You don't, though—not after what you've seen. You ask him if he's okay and he nods. It's the stress, he says. He tells you he can't take it anymore.

None of you can. You all hate each other and the stress grows increasingly unbearable as the end nears. Every time someone screws up, everyone suffers, and they threaten to keep you here longer. The Drill Sergeants continuously tell the platoon how stupid and worthless it is, and after a while you almost believe it. Some privates start malingering in Sick Call (medical attention) and several even say they want out and refuse to train.

The privates who refuse to train are severely punished and have a worse time than anyone, mopping floors all night and receiving special doses of ridicule during the day. One of the quitters threatens that if they give him a rifle or grenade, he'll kill you all. You get more and more depressed as the girl you thought was your girlfriend stops answering your letters.

But the training never pauses. During the sixth week you are tested on everything in the Smart Book. There are no grades in the Army, only pass/no pass—or as the military calls them: Go/No Go. This is due to the fact that in combat there is only dead/not dead. Next, you spend six days of the seventh week in the field, enduring a windchill factor of negative twenty-two degrees, living in floor-less tents and digging foxholes in the mud. It rains the entire six days. Several times during guard duty you doze off and wake to find your face frozen to your rifle.

The final week of Basic is spent cleaning equipment. Finally you hand it all back in and then graduate. There is a mass ceremony. Some lucky guys are able to see their families again.

These are the rough times in your life. They'll get better from here. Even though you're on a bus headed for a warmer part of the country, your mind wanders to what you've learned. The enduring thought in your head is the line "Drive on, private. Drive on."

These are the words soldiers use during trying times to find what the Army calls "Intestinal Fortitude,"—the stuff in your gut that keeps you going. Intestinal Fortitude is what you can rely on whenever you're about to do something you don't think you're capable of, whether it's a push up or a business proposal. You realize that you've got that now.

You didn't think you could survive Basic Training. From the first moment they screamed in your face: "Forget about the college money. You're here to learn how to fight and die for your country!" and you realized with dread, The Army owns me for the next eight years…You were afraid in the back of your mind that you really were as worthless and stupid as they said you were, and you would never get out of this alive. But you did. You passed their tests. You proved them all wrong.

High school football was tougher.

A Modern Marriage Problem

I throw my clean laundry on the bed; maybe I'm lazy, maybe it makes me think she's beside me when I sleep.

I miss my wife. She's gone back to Oregon to finish her degree—my job is holding me in El Paso. It's the army, not a job I can quit.

This is how your life gets wrapped up in someone else. This is your daily existence as an interaction with someone else—like talking to yourself, like thinking: like every thought has an opposite and equal answer in them.

This is what it's like to be married.

Now it's—it's a phone call and email. It's trying to find in the spaces of silence on the phone line that same intimacy. It's reaching. In every phone call there's a desperation—a tight rope of right words and right subject, to communicate the right feeling every time. Carelessness isn't so easy to fix on the phone, on increasing phone bills and finite resources. There's no time and no space in which to correct mistakes; not the way a touch would. How many words equal the power of touch? And the reasons for this separation are logical and good but what value does the future have to pay for right now? If I were to die today, tonight, she would be far from me—

But life isn't marked by drama. This is a matter of the future we are making together, of her attaining those dreams she gave up to be here with me. She left school when I graduated so we could get married and be together. She sacrificed for me and now I can for her. Because this isn't an easy place for her, not an easy city to find work in or the army an easy culture to fit into. Her dream is the degree and more, all the doors it will open. I won't stand in the way of that.

Do people sacrifice like this anymore? Is this a modern marriage problem? This hurts to the core. This is an ancient marriage problem. We're pioneers. We're explorers. We are like every other couple in history who had to balance love and dreams.

And maybe it's not such a bad thing. Maybe the hurt is a fire to temper us. I have to admit there's a romance in it. There's a tension and a heightened life in the longing that isn't always there in the day to day. We've tasted that. We know what ruts are like—how the process of falling in love must be recognized and pursued or it dries up from the safety of it. Love's a static thing if you let it lock you in, if you numb yourselves in the habit and security of it, afraid of these tests, afraid that any change might cause an upset and ruin it all.

Yeah: conflict drives our lives. The secure way is really the insecure way. Conflict gives us stuff to talk about and stuff to laugh about and shouldn't we seek it out? Shouldn't we create it? Or is this hubris? Are we playing with the divorce statistics, taunting the average, daring the institution to crack under the strain. Pushing it to the limits. Extreme marriage. Marriage Max. We should make a video. But one of her friends told her:

"You know you're gambling with your marriage."

And we got scared.

Are we? Our marriage is a toddler and it's growing, deepening, gaining facets it didn't have before. This is us in this situation. We will be different people at some other time in our lives. Right now: we're making it on a shoestring, honing it down to its essentials. Reinventing and relearning us. We're different people than when we met six years ago. When I was a student and her working. Then we were both students. Then we were both working. Now we're back in the framework where we began: one of us talking about work, one about school. Who will we be in the future? I have no set vision but we must be together. This is the process; this is our life. There are goals in sight but no determined end. Loving her is the hardest and best thing I have ever done.

But I miss her now. I'm the guy by himself at the mall. I'm the guy eating alone. I am the Siamese twin with his sibling removed, the amputee itching at excised limbs. The house is filled with her shadows, with her hints and echoes, her voice just in the other room. But I am alone. I go to work and come home. I sleep on my side of the bed. I am waiting for her. I see the clues of her everywhere: on the walls and in the trash, the arrangement of shoes on the closet floor, a book placed on the shelf, plates stacked in the cupboards. The house is half vacuum, the quiet she left in her wake, the air rippling and slowly settling and I don't want this stillness—I want—

I want the future and I want the present and I can't have both. She must have her dreams or we'll poison our future. For that the present has to pass. Neither of us is happy. Getting back on the airplane after seeing each other is the worst. But we know what must be done, despite the tears and the longing.

Why must choices like this be made?

Office Sex for Dummies

The impeachment spectacle may be over, but the problem of the coed office will continue to plague Americans until we all learn to just get along. Oh, we never will. The male-female dynamic is the driving conflict in our lives, and suggesting that men and women put aside emotion and get the job done might be too much to ask.

Our inability to even deal with the question is proof enough of its immediacy. Nobody knows what to do now that Mr. Starr's done producing all his "facts." Sexual harassment civil suits continue to redefine the office politic, while our military has simply regressed into ruling: "Get caught, spend twenty years in Leavenworth," as if fear could ever conquer lust.

The pitfalls and consequences are widely publicized, especially since we've all had the experience of living vicariously through Mr. Clinton. Yet we continue to mix business with pleasure—AMACOM Publishing has even seen fit to offer a manual on the subject, "The Office Romance: Playing with Fire Without Getting Burned," (with Office Sex for Dummies pending)—like Icarus flying too close to the sun.

Do we think we're sophisticated enough to escape the traps? In his memoir *Travels* Michael Crichton recounts an instance where he thought he was smart enough to test the office sex waters, despite several warnings from his psychiatrist.

"Within two weeks my life was living hell," Crichton writes. "I quickly learned that this cute, large-breasted girl was not for me. I knew it, and she knew it, too. Suddenly nothing worked right in the office: things didn't get done; callers were insulted; appointments were missed; details overlooked…"

He concludes: "I couldn't believe it. Not only had our affair not worked out; now I was going to have to fire her."

Crichton knew it was wrong and he did it anyway. The same could be said of Clinton. So if everyone knows it's wrong, why do they keep doing it?

Chaos and misery could be fun.

Or, the current generation of ladder-climbers just doesn't know sex at work is trouble.

It's not for lack of examples, certainly. I think the problem is social—implicit in the high school mentality espoused by the Cosmo girl and the Details guy, and beautifully demonstrated by the Fox TV programming many of us grew up watching: Beverly Hills 90210, Melrose Place, and Ally McBeal. I'm not blaming television; but the shows suggest that the ideal professional is concerned less with business success than with the ultimate ideal of getting-off in the short term.

High school kids have nothing better to do than develop socially, so 90210 could seem rather harmless when taken by itself. It's the anti-development into Melrose and McBeal territory that makes these examples troubling. The adults on these shows play the same high school games as the supposed teenagers on 90210. The programs cater to progressively older audiences, yet their underlying themes remain the same.

Says critic Terrance Rafferty of Ally McBeal: "Perhaps it doesn't trouble [the yuppie audience] that the heroine's attitude toward the real world of work and relationships is so childish, so petulant; she's constantly disappointed by life's failure to satisfy her expectations of boundless love and unqualified success. I'd hate to think that the series's characters were truly representative of their generation."

I'm thinking: Yeah, they are.

Rafferty suggests that all Ally McBeal demonstrates is how gullible today's young people are for falling for such blatant marketing. Of course, continuously falling into and out of relationships, failing to commit to anything, and viewing a meandering pursuit of fun as a life plan can't hurt the country's GDP; but who's to say the creators of such programming are trying to market anything? Maybe they're just reflecting what's already out there, another—cough—lost generation with no clear steps to give living a sense of development.

Why shouldn't working be like high school? College was, with the addition of unchecked drinking. And now all these young executives, men and women, find themselves in the work force and nobody telling them how to relate to each other, so they do it the only way they know how: sexually. (We've even got a new Fred Savage sitcom, helpfully titled Working, to demonstrate all the office hijinks possible.)

According to AMACOM Publishing: "Office romance is flourishing! One recent AMA survey showed that 80% of workers polled know of or have been involved in an office 'amour'; another revealed that one-third of all romances begin at work. Happily, for all concerned, these relationships are no longer prohibited affairs. In today's enlightened business world, most companies permit workplace relationships—having wisely decided that you can't outlaw love."

But there have to be rules, which author Dennis Powers helpfully outlines while "taking a refreshingly positive look at workplace romances—instead of focusing on sexual harassment concerns."

That darn sexual harassment thingy.

What good is a relationship based in work-commonalities when one or the other of those involved gets downsized, moves onto career number six, or decides they can't take the mad city anymore? Mr. Powers should devote some study to the "lack of real lives" in the current set of hipsters that reduces their sex-search to the adjoining cubicle, when they could be out culling through bars like the rest of their boring generation.

The troubling point to consider in the examples of Clinton and Crichton is that not only were their affairs matters of lust, but they were also matters of power. In both cases the male figured in a dominant position. As the coed work force matures, more and more men are going to find the tables turned.
—The personal is political, a fact impeachment has sloppily proven. Easy or not, these issues scream for definition. The military's answer of "outlawing love" certainly isn't the best.
However, as more males find themselves dominated, rail-roaded and generally used like Kleenex by their female bosses, the collective whining will send the country scrambling for a new set of social norms.
Unless, of course, they're into that sort of thing.

What the Marlboro Man Has To Say

The images say this is an American.

The subject is invariably male. He is six feet tall, though the only scale is via purple mountains in the background or rearing horses. He is lean and weathered with enough youthful edge to make him sexy. He is a man boys emulate and women make an ideal.

His world is the silent outdoors, where skies swim with the pastels of sunsets and sunrises, overcast grays and blues. In that silence he both partakes in and tames nature: navigating a sea of cattle while surrounded by those majestic peaks that most U.S. citizens have never seen.

A real image of the West may exist somewhere in history books, but in the collective unconscious of our nation, the icon of the Marlboro Man has come to symbolize our Western heritage. To see him is to long for simpler days when men and women conquered nature and carved out our nation through sheer willpower.

Our snapshots of him in magazines and on billboards show us that the man of the past partook in many activities. He drove cattle. He broke broncos. He built fences across prairies. He sat at campfires in the evening with his buddies. Sometimes he just walked, lanky as a coyote, with a saddle slung over his shoulder, headed for the nearest bridlery shop.

Despite his raison d'etre, the Marlboro man isn't always smoking. Earlier in his advertising tool career he always sucked a fag—while more recent advertising portrays him as a man of action, a man too busy to smoke tobacco.

If he doesn't even use the product he's trying to sell, why does the Marlboro Man remain such an effective advertising tool for Phillip Morris?

The answer: He has surpassed the realm of advertising and become a mainstay of our culture.

This has happened for a number of reasons.

When Marlboro cigarettes first hit the market, they were a filter-tipped cigarette whose main consumers were women. When Phillip Morris decided to attract the male market, a new advertising campaign was launched to build the image of Marlboro as the cigarette for outdoor men "who came up the hard way." The company used only images of rugged cowboys and tattooed laborers to sell the cigarettes.

In early television commercials, these hard-bitten men would each say something about their outdoor life and explain why they chose Marlboro. Then the Marlboro Man appeared, riding the ranges smoking Marlboro cigarettes. When the ban on tobacco advertising on television robbed him of his voice, the Marlboro Man entered the two-dimensional world of print advertising, which may have only increased his viability as an icon.

The cultural myths behind the Marlboro Man help our society deal with a number of complex issues. Looking at these images from a contemporary viewpoint, we can see that the Marlboro Man helps soothe many of the problems we face in society today. He represents stability. He represents a simpler time when problems could be solved with pure hard work, and a person deserved a smoke at the end of a rough day. He supports and validates masculinity.

As men find it more difficult to define themselves in today's society, the Marlboro Man stands as a testament to what a real man is and always will be. Even if a guy can't lead cattle drives or live in Wyoming, he can smoke Marlboro cigarettes and feel a part of that tradition.

For women the Marlboro Man offers the same escape. He reinforces many of the patriarchal norms boys and girls internalize growing up on television. As a woman's life becomes more complex with career and other demands, escape to the safe, rigid structure that the Marlboro Man reinforces might seem appealing. He represents a set of values and beliefs that seem to be disappearing from our present world.

Maybe a man who smokes Marlboro cigarettes would be less likely to lie than other men?

As other advertising campaigns work from standpoints of blatant sexism, the Marlboro Man remains on the high ground. How refreshing is it to flip through page after page of print advertising that is nothing but swimsuit models and segmented body parts and then find the soothing outdoor images of the Marlboro Man? Mountain ranges, whitewater, charging horses, a flickering campfire. He functions as the antedote to today's hectic advertising regimen.

His myth is the same as that supported by country music. The wild west country music glamorizes no longer exists. But Country Western thrives as a lifestyle supporting the values and beliefs thought to have existed during that time. When the Alternative music circuit weighs people down with whining about the world's problems, doesn't it feel good to change the radio station to songs that are "moral" and easy to understand?

If this myth does exist, does the dominant ideology of our society support it? I believe it does.

One print medium that regularly carries Marlboro advertising is *Rolling Stone* magazine. This is a magazine that is oppositional in nature.

It's content often depicts and even glamorizes troubling elements of our society because it's eager to jump on fringe cultures and move them into the spotlight. Flipping through the magazine can seem like a roller coaster ride for the teens who read it, battering them with complex images and concepts. Until they find the Marlboro Man, and images of what America "ought to be."

No one wants to maintain the status quo in our society more than tobacco companies, who are slowly dying under the pressure of changes in our culture. The Marlboro Man stands as a reminder of what many people see as an American ideal. He is one with nature. He works hard. He appears to be fulfilled.

These are all the things a person should strive for to be happy. To want more social change, for instance, is to introduce unhappiness into what was your uncomplicated life. To learn that cigarettes will kill you is not as important as supporting those practices and beliefs that will keep our country strong and "moral." Through the Marlboro Man, Phillip Morris is able to commodify the values people long for in their lives and sell them as products.

However, the Marlboro Man serves a dual purpose in *Rolling Stone*. The magazine's demographic is a much younger audience with a higher education level than those who might have internalized what the Marlboro Man represents. For this audience, *Rolling Stone* is the dominant ideology. Their world is one of constant opposition to older generations. As they rapidly become the majority and their ideals are incorporated, the Marlboro Man finds himself oppositional. That makes him cool.

In the flow of advertising, the Marlboro Man represents a backwater of relative safety. He moves incongruously across our dazed minds like a cool breeze. As a cultural text he represents inspirational myths and a comforting reinforcement of our internalized ideology.

In the Marlboro Man, advertising agencies have achieved their highest aim: to have a campaign incorporated into culture. But what culture does he represent? Some of the photography used to depict him is stunning and could be called art, but the Marlboro Man is working class all the way. However, this was his aim from the start. As wealthier consumers give up smoking, this image continues to work in the favor of Phillip Morris. Being a "low culture" icon is what made the Marlboro Man so successful. A broader range of people can identify with him and the idealized surroundings he lives in.

Though he fits what I consider the old ideological mold, the Marlboro Man endures because he is oppositional to the new ideology. Smoking no longer fits in the new social structure. Slowly the Marlboro Man finds himself a martyr to the values and beliefs inherent in the old dominant hegemony. So he is able to maintain two cutting surfaces: one as a representative of the old way, and as a rebel faced with the new way.

In our pop culture, these ads don't fit the norm. Rarely accompanied by body copy, they remain mute among all the other screaming voices. A moment of silence in the din of print advertising. They do possess a beauty, a serenity captured in moments of simplicity with nature. These qualities are constant in the advertising campaign.

So these images probably do appeal to both high and low culture. Their ambiguity lends most of their appeal as pop culture icons. Working class people appreciate the honesty and simplicity of the way of life represented. Wealthier people see the ads themselves as beautiful, even classy, things, scenery in magazines.

And how they interpret this text determines how they use it. Will it make them smoke? Probably not. But as I stated earlier, it serves as a subtle, enduring reminder that, hey, life was a little better when we roamed the range and smoked cigarettes. The ads are highly unique, but they slide past the eyes almost subliminally.

The subliminal quality of the Marlboro Man as a pop culture icon is what makes him a complex cultural sign. He represents myths our society holds about masculinity, work ethic, values, racial identity and patriarchy, among others. These signs reinforce the dominant ideology, depending on how the receiver decodes the text. As I explained with Rolling Stone, this ideology is in flux, which lends more complexity to this particular sign. It all boils down to how he is interpreted by any particular audience, which is true of any sign.

What the Marlboro Man represents becomes more difficult to determine when he doesn't play as prominent a role in the advertisement. In a recent issue of *Spin* magazine, a Marlboro ad depicts a large rock formation painted gold by the sun, and in the bottom corner is the silhouette of the Marlboro Man on his horse, looking more like a logo than the subject of a photograph.

This ad does have text, and the words "Welcome to Marlboro Country," are written across a shadow in the picture. Here the Marlboro Man continues to function as a sign, but the sign is broadened. He is merely a reminder. The product being sold is not just his lifestyle, but the great outdoors. The ad attempts to commodify nature, suggesting that Marlboro cigarettes are like the great outdoors. The background of the picture is a panoramic desert stretching away into the distance, giving the impression of unlimited freedom in "Marlboro Country."

Here a beautiful picture becomes a sign selling freedom and nature. Is this immediately recognized by those reading this text? Or does this fit into the overall flow of these images as they reinforce the dominant ideology subliminally? The sign becomes so obtuse that there is no way to make sense of it immediately. Here the Marlboro Man and his world communicate a feeling—whatever feeling the reader wants to inject in the scene.

I think in a way this makes the public's relationship with the Marlboro Man more personal. No one is telling them what he says or feels. He is just there in those wide open spaces. He can represent any number of desires in a prospective consumer. This is another aspect of his stature as a pop culture icon: ambiguity. Anyone can identify with him.

The Marlboro Man is an excellent example of advertising that succeeds based on identification. He represents so many things that it is hard for someone not to find something to identify with. Whenever he is placed in a venue where someone might not like him, such as Spin, he leaves the foreground and sells nature instead. He never really sells cigarettes. This is smart advertising. It has worked for Marlboro for nearly thirty years.

Because the Marlboro Man doesn't sell cigarettes, he must represent something else, a stability we wish we had. For men, he is the man they wish they could be. For women, he is the man they wish they could find. His silence makes him golden. In a sense he is more a mirror reflecting back on society what they want from their culture.

Phillip Morris will undoubtedly stick with this campaign until they're run out of business. It is inexpensive to produce and has a history. He's not Joe Camel appealing to children, except that they might look up to what they think he represents, not realizing that he doesn't really represent anything at all.

He is like all other pop culture icons. We make him real. What he means is up to us.

Interviews

Brian Michael Bendis
is through being crime noir's best-kept secret

The Brian Michael Bendis School of Comic Book Crime has three prerequisites: an ear for dialogue, a sack of nickels for the photocopier, and a troupe of actors and friends unfazed by cops who shove pistols in their faces.

Being an artist is a given.

The actors and dialogue go hand in hand. Bendis, author of *AKA Goldfish* and *Jinx* both out on Caliber Comics, writes his black and white crime noir comic books much like a director storyboards a film. First he writes a script heavy with description and speech, then gets his "characters" together to act out the story and perfect the dialogue, adding all the "you knows" and "likes" that make the talk true to life.

Bendis, 27, then records the process, photographs the actors and uses the resulting "storyboard" to make his books. That's why, like a movie but unlike other comic books, Bendis' work always includes a cast list.

It's typical for Bendis to straddle the line between several different types of media. Each of his books is a frenetic montage of influences and he readily admits that he's a pop-culture junkie.

"When a creator looks outside the art and business of comics for their inspiration, then he or she can do it right," says Bendis. "Comics is a bastard art form, like rock 'n roll is a bastard music form. See, rock 'n roll is alive when it goes to other music sources to build itself up. Comics is the same. It's not purely writing, it's not merely illustration. It's a bastard of the two plus much more. It can take from photography, poetry, film, painting and it can be all of those things. There's no limit."

If he can't draw a backdrop the way he wants, Bendis goes to the city that inspired it, Cleveland—his home and the setting for his work—and takes a picture of the scene. He then photocopies the picture repeatedly until it acquires the faded, dreamy/ugly quality he's searching for and uses that as the setting for his story. He calls the process "Xeroxography." That's where the nickels come in.

Other media come into play especially in the dialogue, which is riddled with pop-reference springboards. A conversation begins on the name of an actor, slides into the movie, might have been the book—but it was all about a crime.

"What really gets me going is supreme conversational dialogue," says Bendis. "People interrupt each other, they break each other off, repeat a word three or four times without even realizing why they did it. So I'm trying to see that in my head as purely as possible and get it on the page."

David Mamet and Richard Price are Bendis' ideals in the area of dialogue, and he notes that they both work heavily in the crime genre.

The presence of crime in Bendis' work is the quality that makes it both real and romantic for the reader. Crime can happen to anyone at any time, he says. It's a fear everyone relates to.

"No," he says. "I'm not a grifter. I haven't done what my characters do. That's what research is for."

He then adds: "But I have had a gun shoved in my face. I know what it's like to be in that situation."

"That situation" entailed Bendis and some friends shooting a cover for one of his books that involved a fake mugging. When the Cleveland PD arrived on the scene and found Bendis, who has a shaved head and admits he "looks like a punk," pointing a water pistol at an actress, they took the initiative to shove him up against a wall while a .38 muzzle kissed his temple.

"It was an experience," he says.

That schism where the romance meets reality is what makes Bendis' work so compelling. He has a clear understanding for both sides, although his love clearly lies with the stylized "Jack Nicholson kissing Faye Dunaway in China Town"-allure of crime noir.

"Crime noir has to be about sex, money and murder," says Bendis. "There has to be a femme fatale that is the embodiment of sex and death. And I'm not talking about big breasts and ankh necklaces. I'm talking about real sex and real death. It's got to have a male lead that has a "why me?" look on his face. And the city—"

The city, he says, is the supporting cast.

The city has to be as cold and dark as a photocopy, with hidden secrets in the fuzzy resolution and faltering black ink. The city is the silent observer, the withheld judgment, the mother that doesn't care what bad games her children play. The city is elegant and cruel, paved by possibilities and littered with the remnants of quickly forgotten tragedies whose ghosts whisper regrets in the alleys and clubs. This is where Bendis' hustlers, gamblers, cops, waitresses and bounty hunters make their money or lose it all.

"Who can resist that?" he asks.

Not Hollywood, with whom Bendis has two deals in production for *AKA Goldfish* and *Jinx*. He dislikes talking about them due to the "flaky nature of the industry." Movie "success" isn't that important to him anyway.

"I admit that I sit at a movie like the *Usual Suspects* and I look at the audience around me and think 'They would like what I do,'" says

Bendis. "Why is it that a bad movie is still more respected than a great comic book?"

He says he got into comics because it is the easiest way to tell a visual story and still retain complete control—not as a stepping stone into movies. Where movies are an intensely collaborative process, a comic book creator has total rein of their vision from conception to execution. Admitting he's a control freak, that aspect of comic books is important to Bendis.

"Success for me," says Bendis, "is creating a book you're proud to put your name on. Success is creating a book you'd want to read. Success is challenging yourself to grow as a creator, to try new things each time out. There are a lot of so-called successes working out there who can't say that's what their doing."

At present, success for Brian Bendis includes moving his monthly title *Jinx*, the story of a female bounty hunter who falls in love with a grifter, from independent Caliber Comics to Image Comics, one of the biggest comic book companies in the United States. The move is an interesting contrast because Image is infamous for its books that rely on gratuitous violence and teenage titillation to sell—both of which Bendis is opposed to.

"You know what?" he says. "If I didn't affect a change, who would? The book isn't going to change. It's still going to be black and white. It's still going to be bi-monthly. It's just that now people will be able to get hold of it."

Gender-Specific, New-Wave, Girl-Powered Punk Rock:
The Third Sex

Okay, here's a joke for you. This girl named Trish walks into a car repair garage needing a number sixteen fuse. Normally mechanics are pretty nice guys, but the one she asks just stares at her and says, "Are you sure you want a number sixteen fuse?"

"Yes," Trish answers.

"That's a pretty rare fuse," he tells her.

"I guess," she says, tapping her foot. "Are you going to give me one?"

The mechanic scratches his head. "Have you got a husband or a boyfriend who can help you put it in?" he asks.

Trish bites her lip.

Attaining a number sixteen fuse, she returns to the van to find her two bandmates, Killer and Peyton, swapping "Are you a boy or a girl?" stories. They all laugh. Fuse in place, they reach their gig on time and rock like fiends.

The punchline? The Third Sex (that's who they are) just don't know how to say yes to opposition. The only thing funny is anybody in their way.

By turning opposition into empowerment, these three strong women have shaped their message into new-wave punk rock. They are also a link in a very real network of girl rockers spanning the U.S. who have learned to rely on each other for the support, emotional and logistical, to speak—hell, shout—their minds in a male-dominated music world. They've taken the stage to stand up for the issues close to them: relationships, women's rights and being gay in a straight world.

It's important to understand that the Third Sex was born from girl power. Trish Walsh and Peyton Marshall, the founders of the band, met during a party at which several influential Portland girl bands were playing, including what is now Team Dresch. "I had always wanted to start a band with other girls," explains Trish, guitarist/vocalist for the band, "but I didn't really know how. I felt really intimidated by the entire process. It wasn't until I had a lot of role models like Team Dresch that I became really inspired to do it. I felt so empowered. I felt that if they could do it, I could do it too."

Peyton and Trish wrote songs, went through several drummers, and even opened for a Bikini Kill/Team Dresch show on the main stage of La Luna in Portland, Oregon. "They had heard us playing in the basement," Peyton says, "and they said, 'Why don't you just come down and play a couple songs before we come on?'"

Trish continues, "And we were like, 'Okay?' So we went up even though we only had three songs. It was the most exciting night of my life. That was when I knew this was what I wanted to do. It was a really girl-powered show, so everyone was really supportive and the energy level was really high." Trish laughs. "We were shaking so fucking hard."

In January of 1995 they met Killer Melford and fell in love with her instantly. "She rocked our world—and our band," Peyton says, grinning. When Killer came on, the band already had a line up of shows even without a drummer. So they told her to just come over and they would work things out, which Killer was more than willing to do. "We told her to just try and keep up," Trish says, smiling.

The band has been rocking ever since, performing shows almost every weekend and producing both a seven-inch single and a full-length album to be released in June. Unlike most bands, they practice every night. "The music is a release for me," Trish explains. Peyton and Killer nod their agreement.

It's Thursday night at the La Luna second stage. The show has been billed as Queer Night and a crowd of about 60 people has gathered for the music. Like all hard-working musicians, the Third Sex walk onto the stage, plug-in, and tune and adjust their own instruments. Tonight Trish is wearing a tight silver shirt with some even tighter black pants; her multi-colored, black/blonde hair is piled high on her head. Peyton walks out with her bass slung low. She's wearing polyester parachute pants and a white dress shirt—a slim piano-key tie completes her new-wave mod. Killer is nearly invisible behind her drum kit except for her big black sunglasses. As they prepare to begin, Peyton and Trish both don sunglasses as well.

The band takes a moment to share glances and shrug at each other, grinning. Stepping up to the microphone, Trish raises her eyebrows and shouts an imploring, "One, Two—One, Two, Three, *Four!*" Killer explodes on the drums and the distortion starts to roll. Throughout the show, Peyton and Trish trade off the vocalist spotlight, even trading instruments for a number. Peyton plays with one foot forward, one back, her slim body leaned away from the bass. With her white/black attire, short ink-black hair and space-age sunglasses, she looks like a member of Cheap Trick circa 1987. While she's playing, Peyton is the essence of cool.

Trish attacks her "RU12?"-adorned guitar with feverish strokes of her pick, wailing into the microphone with her eyebrows sky-high. "I know a girl," she sings, "who thinks that she is dead inside—but I know that she's alive—if I could just reach out and touch her—but she won't let me get that close to her 'cause I'm the lesbian freak..." Then she and Peyton share a moment at the center of the stage, grinning at each other while they slam on their instruments in frantic unison. Halfway through the set, Trish pauses to ask the audience: "If it's true that Portland has the third highest number of lesbians and gays per capita of all the cities in the world, why can't I get a date?" The crowd screams and the Third Sex break back into their music.

The only visible part of Killer, besides her sunglasses, are her arms, long and defined, flashing in the stage lights as she hammers on the drum heads. Her fills are tight, running the band through riff after riff, maintaining the wild pace like a drill sergeant on Benzedrine.

The energy-level is at the roof. The crowd loves them. As the set ends, ten or twelve sweaty people rush forward—boys and girls—to express their admiration. The band is more than happy to oblige.

They're really sort of shy. When I ask for a little personal background they all grin and glance around modestly. We're sitting in the grass at Eugene's Hendricks Park, surrounded by lush rhododendrons and elderly, wandering tour groups. It's a great day: warm sun, cool breeze and soft, dry grass. There's a second of indecision while it's silently decided who will talk first.

Finally Killer laughs and tells me she's from L.A. and has been playing music for fifteen years. She grew up during the L.A. punk explosion when bands like the Germs and X were making waves. Her focus has always been playing drums. After a period of moving around, she settled in Portland, not knowing what she would find, but she was pleased with the scene she discovered and has been happy there ever since.

Peyton isn't quite so talkative. She's been quiet throughout most of the conversation, content to pluck at the grass we're sitting on. She says that she moved from Virginia to Portland five years ago to pursue an

English/Creative Writing degree. Later Trish fills in that Peyton loves writing, good food, martial arts and their runaway cat, Gill.

Trish explains that she's currently a college student, originally from New York. She came out to her family after graduating high school—and afterward was a hard time, so she moved to Portland to have a place of her own. In Portland she found a supportive network of girls and also a cost of living low enough that she could support herself with just a part-time job.

They make Portland sound like a good place.

The music scene that has nurtured and sustained the Third Sex and other girl-powered bands is the result of a natural reaction. It is the result of women wanting entrance into an historically male-only club of musical support and knowledge, and being continuously denied access. This isn't knowledge like that learned in junior high, where all the good girls play flutes and clarinets, it's the path to making electric music—rock music. The male music scene doesn't like women to take that path.

It's not uncommon for club owners to refuse the band shows, saying that they already have two or three "girl-bands" on the bill that month. About that, Trish complains, "Every other night will be normal night. But if the girls are going to play a night, then that night is 'chick night.'" Apparently, there are two types of music in the world: girl music and boy music. Bands with women as members are labeled accordingly by reviewers, venue-owners and even the audience.

"You always see 'You might like this if you're into girl rock,'" Trish says, "but you never see, 'If you're into boy-rock...'" She shrugs and her bandmates smile.

The whole process can be difficult. Trish explains, "When I first started I had a guitar and that was all. I didn't know how to use an amp. It sounds really basic now. But when you're not raised in a culture that promotes women playing electrified music it can be really intimidating."

Peyton adds that its really hard to go into music stores because they don't take women seriously. "They always assume you'll want acoustic strings rather than thinking you play an electric guitar."

It was in Portland that Trish found the network of women musicians who were willing to say, "Okay, this is what you do," and help them to make the music they wanted to make. About the network of female musicians, Peyton says, "It's important to share. You have to put back into the music scene what you take out. I have a friend who is trying to start a solo project, so I try and get her shows, try and give her numbers of people she should call and I go to her shows and support her. It's really hard the first year. You have to fight. You do it even if you're not conscious of it—you do fight. I've fought about it, the mental blocks that told me I didn't have anything to say, or that I shouldn't be on stage or that I'm wasting people's time or I'm not a good musician. Insecurities that I'm going to have doubly [as a woman]."

It's all about supporting each other. Trish adds, "We went on tour last summer and met so many radical girls who were putting on shows and lending radio support and were really into helping each other and giving support and making a culture."

"It wouldn't work," Killer says, "without the people in the little towns contributing in that way. If you look at it from the male perspective, they have their support system already there. There are already guys who help them get shows, whether they're aware of it or not. They trust each other and help each other out. Why shouldn't there be something like that from the female perspective as well? When I first started playing, which was a while back, there weren't that many girl-bands at all. I was inspired by this other girl drummer. The first time I saw this band, I had never really seen a girl drummer play before. I was so amazed by the power of this musician, this woman drummer who was up there and not holding back."

Killer pauses and smiles. She continues, "Some women musicians, particularly drummers—straight or gay or whatever—tend to hold back because they think they won't get dates or that they'll be perceived as lesbian, so they hold back a lot of their energy. Just seeing the power of that woman—I was very impressed. Before then I hadn't even thought about picking up an instrument. But I talked to this woman and she told me to just get an instrument and start playing. That was very inspiring. Back then the network didn't really exist but that's how it started and it's been perpetuating more and more."

Her bandmates nod in agreement.

"If we can play a show," Killer says excitedly, "and inspire some girl to come up to us and go, 'Wow! You guys play hard! I want to do that too.' Pretty soon there will be more girls playing in bands than guys and we won't have to worry about anything anymore."

I fumble around with the "coming out" question and they appear slightly amused by my discomfort. I feel like I'm asking someone I don't even know to explain to me in detail how they lost their virginity. "If you're uncomfortable talking about it," I say, "it's okay." I only ask so that others can draw inspiration from their experience.

"Oh, I'm perfectly comfortable talking about it," Peyton rejoins.

But it's Trish who jumps in. She smiles as she states, "I love being a lesbian. I wouldn't want to be anything else. I think it's awesome. That's one of the things that I love about the music and shows is that I'm able to express that part of my life in a really open way." The other girls nod.

"One of the things that we do as queer musicians," Trish continues, "is make ourselves available to queer kids or really anybody who needs to talk. We try to be role models in a really positive way. I think it's important for queer kids to see other queer people being really happy and excited that they are gay. We always like to get letters. We get letters from around the world from kids who are maybe the only queer kid in their school or aren't sure whether or not to come out to their parents or something. Sometimes it helps just to have somebody to talk to."

"In terms of coming out to your parents," she says, "for every kid it's different. I had a really close relationship with my parents my whole life and when I came out to them it was really hard. I'm really glad that I did it and I would advocate being out to anybody. I also think it's something you should think about. Be prepared for anything. Maybe it's not a good idea to come out to your parents right away if you're depending on them for college tuition—or just financially—if you think they might not be supportive. But keeping stuff in like that is also really hard. It's a tough call and definitely worth thinking about and talking about with someone you can trust."

When Trish finishes, Peyton tells me, "I think it's tough being gay in a really straight world. You have to be strong. You have to be really strong, especially when you're young and still dependent on your parents—there's such a negative image of gays that it makes you want to close up, it makes you feel like you have a disease or something. You feel like there's something horribly wrong with you." She pauses. "I didn't know that I was gay for a long time," she says. "But I always had the feeling that I was different somehow."

"There are a lot of kids who commit suicide over the way they feel," Killer says soberly. "So many teen suicides are related to the fact that teens are confused about their sexuality. They don't think they're normal. It's completely normal—even though a lot of people don't want to see it as that."

"And there are a lot of people out there," Trish adds, "who maybe aren't torn up inside but just don't know what their options are. They never see lesbians or know that they're seeing lesbians; it's not even part of their existence. It's never talked about in the house. I didn't even know what a lesbian was until I left home."

Nodding, Killer continues softly, "When you do meet them, you feel like you're home. There's this overwhelming security inside. You think, 'This just makes sense to me.'"

Trish frowns slightly. "Stereotypes lead people to believe that lesbians are all one way," she says, "that they're all really butch or out to get straight girls. It's really important that people understand that lesbians are just like anyone else. Being a lesbian doesn't make you weird, it just makes you like girls instead of boys."

For my final question, I ask the three of them if there is a way they wish straight people would see gays but don't. By now I've realized that Trish is maybe not the group's spokeswoman—I doubt they could decide who is—but she is certainly the most talkative. She considers a moment and answers: "I wish that straight people would question themselves, question their assumptions and just not make any— assumptions. A lot of people don't think I'm gay because I look pretty femmie. But lesbians are all different kinds of people."

Peyton smirks and says, "I was having a conversation at lunch with some people I work with and one lady was talking about how whenever she tells people she's a soccer player they think she's a lesbian. Another lady there had short hair and she said, 'I know! Everyone thinks I'm a lesbian.' So I said, 'Yeah, me too.' And one of them looks at me and goes, 'Well, you are.' And I'm like, 'Yeah, I know.' Well, the soccer player lady was like, 'You are?' and started looking at me like I was a bug—as if to say: 'Now how did that happen?'" Peyton pulls off her sunglasses and stares at me like a crazy hypnotist.

They all agree that people's perceptions of them irrevocably change when their sexual orientation is revealed. When I say that I don't understand why people do that since I don't think a person's sexuality plays that large a role in their life, Trish replies, "It changes how you interact with all people—on some levels. It's very central to who I am. It's not like I go around thinking about sex 24-7…it's about where I find emotional attachments."

She glances at Peyton, who nods her support. "There are some things that straight people wouldn't even think about that hurt me,"

Trish continues, "well, not necessarily hurt me but make me feel excluded or uncomfortable. Safety is also an issue. I think about my own safety. Am I going to get harassed or beat up in a club if I am affectionate with a person that I like?"

The last story The Third Sex have for me is about a show they played in a "horribly sexist bar" somewhere in Seattle. The place was awful but they had a great time.

Trish laughs as she tells the story. "We just took over," she says. "All these dykes showed up and all these girls and it totally felt safe. The energy level was high and it was a very positive thing."

Peyton adds, "We got in a fight with the owner and he told us to never play his stinking bar again."

"Even though he didn't pay us," Trish laughs, "even when we got kicked out, it was still a really empowering experience."

I see the scene in my head: The girls being forced through the door by some greasy, overweight bar-owner, their instruments in one hand, middle-fingers erect in the other, a crowd of women holding them back.

That's one of the great things about having so many girl-powered bands springing up in today's music scene—it's not hard at all to find a band to entrust with the musical takeover of whatever horrible, sexist place comes into view on the horizon.

Mike Allred:
the skinny on comics' resident mad scientist

You're sitting in Fields Brewery in Eugene, Oregon, when you see comic book creator Mike Allred stride through the doors. You've been told he looks like a super hero but you didn't believe it. He does. His height, Viking style hair and chiseled face make him appear a little forbidding. But when he spots you and walks over with a smile, you realize he's one of the good guys.

Critically acclaimed and highly recommended, Allred's *Madman Comics*, available from Dark Horse Comics, is a work that, besides being completely entertaining, asks all the big questions and provides more than a few answers. Just one issue and you'll be hooked on the adventure, romance, philosophy, mad scientists, pop culture and beatnik bad guys—not to mention the retro artwork.

You feel kind of bad when, toward the end of your conversation, Allred admits today is his birthday. Supremely humble, he tells you not to worry about it. He reflects happily on his wife, Laura, his kids, his artistic accomplishments so far, and the fact that he's only. And you think, Wow.

"If I can be where you are when I'm 34," you tell him sheepishly, "I'll be happy."

            *   *   *

You started out in broadcast journalism, didn't you?
First I was a disc jockey. Then I ended up teaching Television and Film Production at the Air Force Academy. After that I was a TV reporter in Europe and got sent all over Europe—until my comic book hobby became bigger than my broadcast career. That's when we made the leap and came here to Eugene. I've been doing comics full time ever since.

Have you always been into comics?
I read them as a kid, but it wasn't until a friend showed me—in my mid-twenties, I guess—that comic books were very different than I remembered them. I've been a big film fan. I always wanted to make a movie but didn't know how to go about it, how much it would cost. When I saw comics, I realized that—since I could draw, I've always had an artistic background—I could combine my writing skills with my drawing skills and I drew my first screenplay, which was called *Dead Air*.

I've always thought of comics as the poor man's film medium—of course with a lot more stylistic choices…a lot of variety available to comics. Any special effect I want, if I can draw it, it's there. It's a one-man show, pretty much. All of that appealed to me and after I did one, I felt I could do better, and I did it again and did it again. Before I knew it, it became a career.

What led up to Madman?
I had been doing some very esoteric, strange, experimental work. In Europe I thought of the title Graphique Musique. On a trip to Paris there was a music store and a graphics shop right next to each other—

graphique musique. I thought, "What a great title." It summed up what I felt about comics at the time: it was graphic music.

So I decided to make a book called Graphique Musique. I was published by Slave Labor Graphics. Then I went to a publisher called Caliber. I spelled it phonetically: *Grafik Muzik*. I used that as an umbrella title. I would be able to tell any kind of story I wanted, in any kind of style I wanted—so I was really just stretching. It got a lot of great criticism and was very successful critically but what was might be regarded as a minor cult hit in the industry. So you're more likely to have heard about it than to have actually seen it. It's like a treasure hunt to find any of those issues.

I've got three kids who are eleven, nine and almost three. At the time the two eldest were becoming school age and wanted to take my work to school for show and tell. You know, "My Dad writes and draws comic books." Well, the work—not that it was necessarily inappropriate for children—it wasn't anything that would interest them or impress them; very avante guard type stuff. So I started thinking about what I loved as a kid and I realized that the industry was largely made up of grim titles, dark and morose.

A lot of the stuff I loved as a kid was intelligent but it was also fun. I thought that was sadly missing. So I thought about doing something that would be colorful and fun and exciting, but also thought-provoking—so I combined my more mature ideas with a more all-ages look.

I took a character named Frank Einstein, which was my favorite at the time simply for the costume on him, and was originally going to call him *The Spook* out my affection for Will Eisner's *Spirit* but then later decided to call him *Madman* after *Catcher in the Rye*. Holden Caufield, the protagonist in *Catcher in the Rye* constantly used the phrase 'madman,' almost like a swear word.

So I called it Madman and it was first published by Tundra which was kind of an Apple Records for Kevin Eastman [creator of *Teenage*

Mutant Turtles], a creative outlet and kind of a stronghold for creators to be treated right. Kevin gave me a great start.

Fortunately it did really well. Then Kevin wanted to do creative stuff again and sold Tundra over to Kitchen Sink Press. That allowed me to look for the best deal and Dark Horse Comics—where I'm friends with and is now my editor, Bob Schreck and Mike Richardson, creator of *The Mask* (before there was a movie before there was the comic book)—and it seemed like the natural place to go. I felt like they would support me and I trusted them.

We started the title over, calling it *Madman Comics*, and it's done incredibly well. It's one of the more successful independent comics. And of course I'm very happy about that.

Comic books seem underrated in their literary value. Do you think there should be a, say, Comic Book Literature 101 at the University?

There are universities with courses on Tom Cruise. But, yes, absolutely. It's a vastly underrated medium. I can speak from an intellectual background and that's more than true. This is something I discovered as an adult. It's very valid. It's a completely unique medium. It's the only one that does combine art and literature in a narrative structure.

Lack of ability to break into any mainstream success as an art form due to its genre—the most successful comics are super hero comics. Fortunately I've worked out sort of a compromise to that.

My character isn't really a super hero. He doesn't have any super abilities. But he's in a costume. I kind of use the genre to my advantage and tell stories that aren't your usual comic book adventures.

When it first started out there were great adventure scripts, soap opera scripts, romance scripts, mystery scripts, crime-drama. The greatest comic book company ever was E.C. They created *Tales From the Crypt*, *Haunt of Fear*, war comics. They kind of got out of the water when the other companies, jealous of their success, I believe, created the comic book code—sort of censoring the more adult aspect of the way comic books were headed. That's what made it a children's medium and we've been fighting that image ever since. Mostly through underground comics which really went the other way—bordering on pornography most of the time—until the mid-eighties when independent comics finally broke out with people like Harlan Ellison writing. Still, the majority of them are super hero comics. But if there was more attention paid to it, more encouragement given to the books that are trying to do something different then the medium would advance drastically.

I sort of see them as portable movies, where you can freeze the time, freeze moments in a film and roll them up and stick them in your back pocket. That's where I come from with comics. There's a lot of encouragement to try and make [comics] collectable. It's one of the cases where our industry is slitting it's own throat.

There's no other entertainment medium where, if something is successful all of a sudden it ends up costing more and it's harder to find. If, for instance, a film is successful—take Pulp Fiction—they make more prints, they put it in more theaters. With comics, if they become successful, everybody hordes them, puts them in plastic bags and sticks them in boxes, hoping that the value will increase some more so they can turn around and sell them. As a creator of comic books, I want people to read them! So a lot of the stuff is crap, because there's no incentive, no encouragement, to write and draw good stories if they're just going to be put in a bag and stuck in a box somewhere. That's a trend that really, and hopefully, will die.

Do you have any control over getting your comics reprinted?
None at all. A lot of my comics are very collectible but most of them [are that way] for the right reasons. They were low print runs because that's all myself or my publishers could afford.

What have you learned since you came into this business?

A million things. How the market works, what their tastes are, how the retailer system works and what kind of readers I have. For the most part, I try to have an all-ages audience. If I go to a show or a store signing, I'll have seven year-old kids wanting their books signed, I'll have eighty year-old grandmothers wanting their books signed. There's a real strong college audience. I'm really proud of that—that my work is entertaining for everyone. There's nothing I'd be ashamed to have a seven year-old read and at the same time it's at an intellectual level that someone at the college level will be able to read.

There is quality literature in the stories and well-rounded characters. It's not just catering to juvenile audiences. I do it for me first and I hope I'm also doing something my kids are going to enjoy and what that makes for is something that most people like. I feel that's lacking in all entertainment. There's very little entertainment that an entire family can go to and all equally enjoy it and get something out of it. Right now Universal Pictures is making a movie [of *Madman*], and I am a little worried about that. So far, on paper I have creative control but you hear horror stories about losing that all the time.

Did you write the script?

I wrote the screenplay and am being given the highest consideration to direct it based on my past television and film production experience. I actually took some of my option money and shot a low-budget feature film myself here in Eugene. To show them "Look what I can do," you know? And with [Universal's] support and budget, I can make the most authentic and faithful adaptation from comic book from screen you could get.

Tell me about the film you just shot.

It's called *Astroesque* and we're editing together the rough-cut right now. I really tried to do everything. I really like being involved in every aspect. With *Astroesque*, I've already painted artwork for a movie poster, that will be in the next issue of *Madman*. With any sort of theatrical release, even if it's just at the Bijou, we're going to put up the posters.

Have you chosen any actors for the Madman *film?*
No. We're still in the story stage, putting the polish on the screenplay. It's a very slow process.

The movie concept has had a lot of trouble getting off the ground, hasn't it?
When *Madman* was first published, it was an option for a film. Then the production stalled because they had to put more money into a Charlie Sheen movie called *The Chase*. I don't know if you've ever seen it or heard of it—but that was actually the best thing that could have happened to me because the comic book became more successful after that. It got picked up as a Universal Pictures film. If it ever gets made it will be an "A" film. A lot of films get stuck in development forever and often are never even made. So, they've got three years to make it. I get paid every year for three years. If they don't make it—eventually, after filming *Astroesque*, I'm already planning to make another film with my friends. We've got real aspirations to great things and make more films. And we'll do that one way are the other.

Ultimately, if *Madman* doesn't get made at Universal, I may end up making it myself. In the meantime, there are other things I want to do, other stories I want to tell.

Stories

We Have Rules

My town is a melee of marriages and pregnancy, the last stand of Toyota lift kits and asphalt licking low-riders sniffing around the high school. In my town empty lots are dance clubs on Saturday nights—exploding with honking, yelping and bass systems out-thumping each other like a tribal ritual. In my town "Where's the party?" is hello and "Who can buy beer?" and "Where's still selling?" echoes as night wears on and that all-numbing beautiful buzz starts fading into Monday's throbbing reality. It's "Who's fucking who?" and "Who got away?" and "Gawd, can you believe her?"

Sure, I believe her. She and her new husband have rules about how they fuck someone else. Rules make it safe, see? But I remember when she was young—fifteen—and seemed so fresh, surrounded by that diaphanous swarm of girls like gold butterflies in afternoon sun.

Floating.

Match rules with memories like this, driving around in the oily Saturday night watching the cars draw to this and that parking lot nexus, lost and empty for each other. Get in line behind the Xerox copies, this bland mass of need with its sitcom souls force-fed Wal-Mart and raised in this town where it seems no one really wants to live.

—Drive around past this part time job and that video store where the girls rush out in their name tags to flirt with the boys in their tall trucks with the doors open. All of them leaning down with crooked smiles and lips swollen from tar-thick chew, so hot in their backwards baseball caps and flannel shirts.

"He's okay, he dated her—"

"Sure, she's friends with—"

Safety there. And somewhere somebody puts a match to this or that and inhales as deep as their emptiness can hold and holds it for a—an hour's warbled escape between twisting walls and flashing fake emotions, slips out thin through pursed lips and runs from a home somewhere and maybe a mom and dad. I remember when two sets of Christmas gifts seemed like such a great idea.

And now I don't want anyone's free shit.

Just drive around hands hot gripping a steering wheel that won't lead me anywhere. Around and around this street, past the park where I found needles as a nine year-old and the junior high with it's low ceilings and knee-high drinking fountains—until finally you'll be sucked into a parking lot just like everyone else. Even you, college boy, because ultimately you and they all know that you'll never get away, not in your heart where the statistics ring true. And accepting who you are is accepting the rules, rejecting those foolish ideals you once upheld when you foolishly hoped you were different. Getting away seems so far away anymore and day to day is eating your life in hungry gulps every time you turn around. And looking back hurts anymore. You had such important dreams.

Boredom and fear built my town.

Shake off that parking lot because there's a party somewhere. Spin the wheel and point the nose of this car into Saturday night—dive— and now there's a backseat full of girls to take somewhere into the haze, reeking of designer impostors and flashing those billboard t-shirts tight across their tight chests. Smiling into your rearview, kissing the air with cherry lips, flashing those shaded eyes as hungry as wolves, hard as dollars. I remember how pure they all used to be. We all had naivete as our get out free card, armored against life. But now it's worn through and nobody accepts innocence as an excuse anymore, like last summer's hit song.

If only I could have found just one girl and lifted her above all this, and we could have kept each other free of it, we could have saved one another from those bored destructions and murmured breakdowns. We could have done something real—something other than another ride down this black road with a yellow snake winding side to side in the center. Crack a beer and nail it down. Laughing and the bouncing top-forty.

Driving.

Driving around.

Real estate around the lake is booming and above the golf course beautiful cardboard houses rise like mushrooms at night. The schools—not great but more money from people like you will change that. That's how those things change. You ask about the bad part of town, glancing around as though anywhere could be bad. Security system a good idea? No, nowhere here is bad like on TV, anyway. Maybe a rifle now and then. Maybe a drunk fool. But this is Nowheres-ville, man. No place to worry yourself about if you're from somewhere else. This is the easy shit, the good life, the salad land, man. Nothing's hard here.

That's why we can't leave.

Interludes, interludes, that's all you get: join the Army, flunk out of college, land back here where everything feels better. Mom and dad missed you and so did we. The parking lots aren't the same without you and the high school girls—oh, man the high school girls. We get older but they just stay the same.

Did you make that up? Shit, man. That's pretty funny. You're pretty funny.

And I remember that messed-up morning, that broken New Year. When Dad just sat in the living room and announced, "Last night I told your mother I don't want to live here any more," And then followed it with, "There—now we're a statistic."

As though the joke could absolve him of part of this pain. As though, as on TV, he could open his eyes to an aw-shucks smile and tussle my hair. And I would be nine again, with syringes from the park asking, "Mom, what are these?"

"Drop those, for God's sake!"

For God's sake, Dad wants to leave. And we all just sat there staring at each other in the most miserably honest light I think we had ever experienced. Now that all the denials we had maintained so faithfully for so long (fishing trips, camping trips, Boy Scouts, high school football: *go hard or get out!*) had suddenly failed and I had to do something 'right.' I had to just put away anger and do something, lift those shields back into place, struggling to lift them alone somehow, glancing around, Dad's face and wringing hands—

Yeah well fuck you! my brother said slamming the door and getting away.

And I just sat there.

Sat there.

Thinking that running was wrong and that there was something I could fix, something I didn't have to run away from but could face somehow, that denial worked after all, maybe, just like they'd taught me—

At least he acted, moved

shouted!

that you couldn't hurt me anymore while I just sat there.

Sat there hearing that last night he said he didn't want to live here anymore and suddenly two sets of presents at Christmas didn't seem as grand an idea as Dan Parent made it seem in fourth grade, and all those damn G.I. Joes he had spread all over his room, even the damn rare Cobra Commander, every one of them was a denial and only now did I understand how ugly those offerings were compared to what I used to have. We used to have.

If only I could find one girl and lift her above all this. If only I could do it right and point that steering wheel out of here and past the weekend into something important and real. We could help each other stay right, get away.

"Oh, you!" she murmurs, one of four in the backseat, one with a leg half out the window, mini skirt hitched up her thigh, a flash of gold panties. This isn't bad, this boredom against the night, really. Really, these are fun girls and this is a good time and really I'm lucky to have times like these. Her cherry lips ease across the edge of my ear, billboard chest soft on my shoulders and somehow nothing seems real and I can float away from my grip on the steering wheel and scream through the roof of the car at this anger growing, this hatred consuming me, knowing all the while that the angrier I become, the less I can say, and the more I sag against the wheel.

The higher I build this black wall of anger like an inversion of the growing hole inside of me, lifting its vacuum into the sky, blotting out the sun, spreading its tattered black wings to beat against everything easy and beautiful and vaguely pure, my ragged piss-stained flag, flaunted for no one to see—the less I can say.

Only hunch over and accept these lips on my ear, these fingers in my hair. And drive. And later, fumbling in the dark: the long spread of that backseat against her eager eyes, the reflection stretching in her irises. And when I can feel her but I can't feel her, I truly believe this isn't so bad, that we have rules for how we do it with each other and if only I could extend this concept. If only I had a condom for my life. If only I could feel half-way and never hurt.

If only I could shout.

"That feels so good," she says.

The Wall Mirror

Quiet now. At the hospital there had been beeps and rolling carts, clicking pens and the hollow echo of voices paging doctors. Now the night slid past the car windows in smooth black waves, segmented by yellow street lamps gliding up the windshield.

Brian held the wheel with both hands and let the road lead them home. It was four in the morning and he was tired. He didn't want to think about the work coming in three hours.

He glanced at Megan but she was dead to him. She held herself in the blanket he had torn from their bed five hours earlier and stared through her black eyes. Her skin was pale as moonlight. One lock of hair divided her wide forehead.

She sniffled and he turned up the heater.

Later he pulled into the driveway and went around the car to open her door for her. She accepted this and walked past him toward the house, huddled in the blanket. He followed, searching through his keys.

Brian switched on the kitchen light and squinted against the glare on his sore eyes. Megan went to the table and sat down. She stared at the wooden napkin holder in the center of the table.

Brian stood watching her. Then he put a hand on the refrigerator and leaned his head against the cool metal. His wife had her back to him.

"Excessive vomiting?" the doctor asked.

"Not that I've noticed."

"Does she seem depressed lately?"

"I don't think so," Brian said.

"Have you noticed any changes at all, Mr. Trenton?"

Changes.

Brian felt the floor heave suddenly but realized his knees were collapsing under him. He caught the hard corner of the refrigerator and balanced himself. When he saw that her back hadn't moved, that she hadn't registered his fall, Brian pushed away and moved down the hallway to the bathroom. Inside he gripped the sink and stared at himself in the mirror.

"Is this some kind of suicide attempt?"

"I don't think so," the doctor said. "But I can't be certain. Mr. Trenton, does your wife have an eating disorder?"

"What?"

"She said all she took recently were diet pills."

They pumped her stomach. Twenty times the recommended dosage. Baby? Twenty times?

"Your wife is acutely dehydrated, Mr. Trenton. I think that's what caused the fainting spell."

"That could be anything, right? Not enough water?"

"Have you noticed her using laxatives excessively?"

He stared at the mirror before knocking his face out of focus by opening the medicine cabinet. Brian studied the white shelves. Tylenol. Midol. Advil. Comtrex. Milk of Magnesia. Ex-Lax.

Green bottle with a white label. He selected the bottle and turned it in his hand, reading the label. He opened the cap and shook a few pills into his palm. Then he dumped them all down the sink.

Lists of things he should have noticed, billboards he should have read. Only a week ago, he recalled their conversation as he lay on the bed watching her dress for dinner out. Her frown in the mirror.

"I look fat."

"You don't look fat," he said. "You look great."

"I'm fat. How can you look at me?"

"You're beautiful. Look at me, Megan. You're so beautiful to me."

She only glowered in the mirror, ignoring his reflection beside her.

"You're blind."

His fatigue had a brittle edge and it was rising, scraping inside his head. Brian left the medicine cabinet hanging open and went into the bedroom. Clicking on the lights he stood in the doorway and searched silently for her private spaces. His eyes fell on the bottom drawers of their dresser.

The drawer screeched as he wrenched it free and flipped it upside down. Lingerie fell on the carpet and Brian pawed through it. Finding nothing, he reached for the lowest drawer. This one was heavier. Dumping it revealed books, photo albums, empty bottles of perfume, letters, her high school yearbook, her college diploma.

Three red and yellow boxes of diet pills.

He grabbed them up. They were light but stubborn to tear open. Brian ripped the first package apart and studied the shiny foil blister pack and its rattling red and yellow capsules. He turned back to the packaging and read the instructions, indications, side effects. His eyes burned into the woman in the swim suit on the front of the box.

"She eats. She eats dinner with me every night. I work days, so I guess I don't know if she eats then. But—I don't know."

"You're wife doesn't work?" the doctor asked.

"No, we—I just got a new job. We just moved here for it and she hasn't found anything yet. She's been looking."

"How long?"

"Four months now, I guess."

Since they had come here, it seemed that instead of growing closer, he was losing her.

Megan looked up at him slowly when he threw the pills on the table in front of her. Her eyes were black holes. She looked at him as if he had hit her.

"What are these?" Brian asked.

"Pills."

"Why do you need these pills?"

Megan lowered her face and squeezed her eyes closed. Tears filled her eyelashes. "Because I'm fat," she said.

"You are not fat."

She didn't look at him, but readjusted her grip on the blanket around her shoulders.

Megan cried out as he grabbed her arm and pulled her to her feet. Halfway down the hallway she struggled, clawing at the antique radio. Its hollow body cracked as it hit the floor, a gasp in the quiet house. Two steps away, Megan's forearms moved in awkward jerks against him, as if each movement expended a deep reserve of energy. She sobbed, hitting his chest, scratching his face. Then she surrendered, slumping against him as he pulled her into the bedroom.

Brian jerked her in front of him before the wall mirror and pulled the blanket free. A second movement tore the neck of her nightgown and revealed one pale breast to the mirror.

She resisted. But he succeeded in ripping the rest of the gown from her body and then he held her with both hands.

"Look at yourself," Brian said.

Megan turned her face away, clenching her eyes closed. Her cheeks were streaked by tears.

"No."

"Look at yourself," he roared, and forced her chin.

Megan refused to open her eyes.

"You don't understand," she said. Her chest jerked with sobs.

"You're right, I don't understand," Brian said, shaking her. "I love you. I love you, Megan. I tell you how beautiful you are to me, how much I want you, and still you eat those pills. Why are you doing this? What am I doing wrong?"

Her voice was muffled: "It's not you."

"What is it then?" he demanded. "Who are you doing this for, if it's not for me? You would do this to yourself?"

She wouldn't answer.

Brian closed his stinging eyes and focused them again on the mirror. He saw that her arms were splotched scarlet from his grip. He relaxed his fingers and really looked at her, looked at the combination of the two of them.

Brian saw himself, eyes bloody. Megan sagged in his grip. He moved his eyes down her body slowly, studying collar bone and belly button as intently as he had read the medicine labels. She looked no different to him. He felt a stirring of desire and suddenly he wondered if she wanted him to make love to her.

"Don't look at me," she murmured, crying.

Brian stared at the mirror. He blinked and looked at her bowed head. Kneeling slightly, he picked her up and held her against his chest. Her face fell against his neck, smearing his skin with hot tears. She was so light that suddenly he felt a sob well in his throat and his eyes blurred, burning.

"Megan," he whispered. "Oh, Megan."

He looked at the sight of himself holding his wife in the mirror. He looked at the line of her bare calf and how graceful her neck was with her face turned toward him. He looked at the bandages inside her arm from the IV drip.

He looked at his own progressing belly, his retreating hair.

Brian turned slowly and walked to the bed, lowering her into the covers. He kissed her forehead before turning out the light.

*   *   *

Megan tried to swallow and gagged instead. The stomach pump had made her throat ragged and the reflex left a tang of blood in her mouth. So she stared out the car window at the images surfacing from the strange dark of this unfamiliar route home from the hospital. Back to their new home in this new place she had come to live in with Brian, requirement of his new job. Of course there was more money, which meant nicer drapes and a new washer and drier set—but she had been perfectly happy with the old drapes in their old two bedroom apartment. Now they had a house.

Out of the dark came the neon glow: *Live Nude Dancers!* And she wondered what dead nude dancers looked like.

She glanced at Brian but he was intent on the road, both hands on the wheel. She sniffled and snuggled deeper into her blanket. In the edge of her vision she noted that he turned the heater up. A warm wind blew on her face from the vent.

But it felt too hot, so Megan pressed one side of her face against the cool window and tried to define the line down her face where cool and warm met, dividing her into two pieces. The cheek against the window was the cool side of her self, and it was sliding away into the dark outside, with the Strip Club signs and street lights glowing as they passed. She imagined herself flowing away into the dark like a piece of paper lost in the wind of passing cars on the expressway, drifting and looping and dancing wherever the exhaust might take her. Maybe she could fly high enough to catch a wind, and then a jet stream, and then she could disappear in the gray clouds making a halo around the moon. Cold and clean as white toothpaste or Cool Whip.

The warm side of her reached uselessly for Brian. She felt as if the hot air formed a wall between them, pushing them apart in stifling gusts, choking her and making him more distant. The car was growing hotter. She felt the engine grinding and the wheels grating against the asphalt. She saw Brian's white knuckles on the steering wheel. His tension was like a taut wire. The were on high wire act and she feared they would fall.

The road slid by. They were leaving the hospital.

And she wondered what all this was about. She had taken some diet pills. A few diet pills and then gone to sleep. Next, she remembered Brian waking her, his face moon-white. She watched him rip the blanket she now wore from the bed and then she was in his arms and then in the back seat of the car, the material rough against her cheek, listening as he changed rumbling gears like a race car driver. The hospital: on her back watching the ceiling lights flash by, the nurse shoving the plastic pump down her throat, like an impossibly swollen twisty straw. Gagging forever. People murmuring over her like bees buzzing.

Quiet now. The lights slid by, surfacing from the dark, floating past. Street signs. Traffic lights. Other faces ghostly in cars alongside in this slow silent regatta…of lives racing down yellow-trimmed lanes. How close they all were, she thought. How dependent upon trust was this road system…what if she just wrenched the wheel? Reached out and jerked the car sideways in the street and smashed their car into an iris of wrecked metal, split open their cocoon to the night air?

Would Brian frown then? Would he notice her? His presence seemed swollen in the small space of the car, pressing her against the cool glass, forcing the warmth out of her skin until she had no recourse but to escape through the glass into the cold, where the people on the street corners lived their lives in this wild new city, so much bigger and angrier than what she had ever known.

They were parked.

Megan lifted her face and saw their new house dark and silent outside the window. Brian was opening his door. He came around the car to open her door, and she thought she wouldn't be able to move—until her support swung away from her and the cold air reached inside the car and grabbed her. She swung her feet out and stood, turned without looking at Brian and walked toward the house. She heard him close the car door and begin searching through his keys. She recognized the familiar jangling sound: the same sound she heard when she was sitting in the living room and, coming home after work, he thought the door was locked. In the three little windows at the top of the door, she would see the top of his head, and she could almost feel his bulk against the door, poised to press into the space she had been creating for herself all day alone—the keys would jingle—and the lock would click and roll and the door would swing open. He would come in with his head bowed, before looking up to see her, and he would always ask: Why didn't you open the door?

It was unlocked, she would always answer. She took comfort in this. Because as long as he cared that she hadn't opened the door—when in fact all she wanted was to bask in the moment of him wanting to enter their house—she knew he was coming home. Brian was coming home.

She loved Brian in a way that terrified her. Megan felt that without him she would cease to exist. He was the baseline of her life: more so in this new place. She had nothing but him to connect her with her old life, nothing but him to prove that she was even real. She couldn't even trust mirrors anymore. She knew she could fool herself, if necessary, into believing she was there. She needed Brian to come home and be angry with her or happy with her or anything at all, to prove that she existed in this world. She couldn't talk to her mom. Her college friends had disappeared into their own lives. She felt like a ghost.

Silly diet pills, she thought, waiting for him to unlock the door. They were food, that was all. Wood to keep her burning. Just like speed, she and her friends had joked in high school. Keep you cooking all day long. Running on a Diet Coke and diet pills. Thanks, but I'm okay.

She couldn't recall how many she had taken before going to bed. She was hungriest in the middle of the night, when she knew Brian was asleep beside her, and she woke up with the black hole inside her aching to be fed. Endless, tireless black hole. That was the only reason she had taken those diet pills. Just to feed that hunger screaming inside her from her toes to her fingertips.

He had said he woke up and she wasn't breathing. But she didn't see how that was possible.

Now the kitchen light was glaring in her eyes. Megan sat down at the kitchen table. There was another reason, too: she didn't want to recognize this reason, though, because it was selfish. And their future depended on this job Brian had now—from here he could transfer anywhere. He was doing just the type of programming he loved, he said. Was it so important that she couldn't find a job, then? Wasn't he making enough money for them both?

The first interview they said she needed more experience. She could accept that. The second interview wasn't a panel but one man. A man named Dave in his mid-forties, whose eyes kept sliding down her body when she talked. Megan knew the exact cadence of his eyes. They fell from eye-contact to her lips, then to her chest, then to her crotch, then her legs, his desk, and back to her eyes. He might throw in a glance at the wall for good measure. This went on for half an hour.

She didn't think much of not getting that job. But when the third interviewer gave her the same treatment, this time sitting beside her rather than behind a desk and actually reaching over at one point to pat her knee, she wanted to scream inside.

And when she didn't get that job, she could only assume it was because she wasn't pretty enough. Sitting at home all day wasn't helping. She tried to go for walks. She wanted a puppy but Brian wouldn't have it. Her pants didn't fit anymore.

She ached inside.

Brian had gone somewhere. Now he was back with a package of the pills in his hand, all mangled.

"What are these?" he demanded.

"Pills."

"Why do you need these pills?"

Megan lowered her face and squeezed her eyes closed. She felt tears fill her eyelashes because she knew she had hurt him, but she hadn't meant it to be that way.

"Because I'm fat," she said.

"You are not fat," he asserted.

He said it as if by making that statement he could fix how she felt in one fell swoop. But he hadn't been sitting at home for four months. He hadn't seen the eyes of those men as they studied her breasts that were too small and her fat calves, her round belly. She had been pretty only a year ago. She knew that. If only she could get back there.

Instead he grabbed her. She gasped, surprised by his violence. She didn't start to fight until halfway down the hall, when she was already crying uncontrollably. He didn't understand. He had somewhere to go, something to do, people to talk to. He didn't wait until he heard keys jangling outside the door.

She tried to hit him but it was no good. She loved him and hated him all in smashing waves. She felt as if she were lost in a vast ocean, fighting against uncaring currents: her life spiraling away. This wasn't where she had thought she would be. He wasn't who she thought he would be. How could he be so blind? Why couldn't she talk to him? Where had this wall come from?

Megan tried to hit the wall but her fists felt like pillows and they fell short. Instead she sagged against him, because at least he cared enough to fight her, until he lifted her in front of the big wall mirror in their bedroom.

"Look at yourself," Brian said.

She refused to look at herself. Again he surprised her by grabbing the throat of her nightgown and ripping it half down her front. With another movement he left her naked. But she wouldn't look. She knew what was there. She had studied the troughs and ridges of her body for hours, pulling and pushing, willing herself to be different, to be smaller, to not seem so distorted and disgusting. Did the mirror show another world? Was she really so horribly fat?

"No."

"Look at yourself," he roared, and forced her chin. His strength hurt her. She had never thought him capable of this.

"You don't understand," Megan said. She couldn't explain to him. Being in this place was too important. She hated herself for taking too many pills.

"You're right, I don't understand," Brian said, shaking her. "I love you. I love you, Megan. I tell you how beautiful you are to me, how much I want you, and still you eat those pills. Why are you doing this? What am I doing wrong?"

"It's not you."

"What is it then?" he demanded.

"Don't look at me," she murmured, crying.

He knelt and lifted her in his arms. She knew she must be too heavy. She felt him strain under weight.

"Megan," he whispered. "I love you, Megan."

She let one IV scarred arm fall away from him. But he wouldn't let her fall. So she turned her face into his shoulder and let her husband carry her to the bed. She was tired now. Her throat hurt and she was tired of crying.

Megan felt him kiss her forehead. But his hands were dumb on her skin. She wanted to sleep now. He didn't understand.

She turned her back to him, and listened as he stood over her a moment. She felt him sit on the bed beside her. She wanted to imagine his face in his hands. But she couldn't look at him to see. Her husband might have been smiling, she didn't know. She pressed her face into her blanket, catching a sob. Then she rolled over and wiped her face, looking at Brian.

His tears were silver in the dark.

The Springfield Girl

My first week at the university I went to a party with my best friend Ron at a complex beside the Carl's Jr. on Franklin. The apartment overlooked a parking lot and its balcony was directly across from the upper story of a fraternity. Ron liked a girl who lived in the apartment. The girl had been unequivocally described as "weird" but Ron searched for a second before calling her simply "scared." He liked to find girls he could show something—he did it unconsciously anyway. She seemed to fit his bill.

The apartment was reached by two flights of rain-slick stairs and consisted of two bedrooms, a somewhat large living room and the kitchen. The balcony was the best feature—it was reached by ducking through a screen door that didn't have its middle section of screen anymore. That's where all the smokers were. Since she smoked that's where we ended up. Ron searched her out as we passed through the front door and caught that first wall of questioning turned faces—that first break where you're either intimidated by the room or drive through. These people were the type we liked to call hipsters, coffee-house people. They listened to British music and wore thick black glasses, had spiky black hair and used words like "mod" and "post-structuralism." Most of them were still in high school. So we drove through.

On the balcony was a girl in an Army jacket and knee-high go-go boots. She thought she was funny because she had a Coors Light in one hand and kept pointing out how funny it was that she was drinking Coors.

Ron knew a few of the people there. He found his girl, Jenna, and introduced me. I didn't see where they got their weird from because she looked like the most normal person there: just wearing jeans and a sweatshirt, brown hair in a pony tail. She had the cuffs of her sleeves pulled over her hands and her hands pulled tight against her chest, pushing her chin forward to suck on the cigarette held in two fingertips peeking from the sleeves. She took big drinks from a wine cooler sitting on the railing.

Ron led off by telling her if she drank the cooler real fast it would make her feel happy.

She smiled. "I've tried that trick."

A tall thin boy in a chair beside me told her to smoke the cigarette all the way down. "There's heroin in the filter," he said. "It's a tobacco industry secret."

The skinny guy's name was Stephen. He talked about bands like the Stone Roses and London Suede. When he went into the kitchen and came back with an oven-bake chicken pot pie, he spent a few minutes extolling the virtues of pot pie as the perfect food.

Jenna was fairly easy going although she kept leaving the balcony at strange times, in the middle of Ron talking about something, dipping a little to show the crowd that she wanted through, hands still clasped against her chest. Then she would come back to where we were leaning against the railing and light a cigarette, ask him to go on. She explained later that she probably had the smallest bladder in the world.

For a while we all became interested in an older guy who someone had divulged was engaged. A girl stared at him and said, "God, I couldn't even imagine being engaged right now."

He acknowledged her and shrugged.

"How long have you been with her?" she asked.

"Three years," he said. "It'll be three and a half when we're married in July."

"Aren't you scared that she's not the one?" Jenna asked, poking her head forward.

"Sure," he said. "But I love her. And I'm graduating soon and it's time for us to get our lives going. I mean, yeah, I worry that things will go wrong and everybody tells me we should do something else, wait longer. But I feel that if you truly love someone, you shouldn't be afraid to jump. Because that's what it is. I could be half-ass all my life or I could jump. And I choose to jump." He took a drink of his beer.

"Plus, you know," he said. "The idea doesn't fill me with dread or anything. It makes me feel relief—sort of like, finally. Finally I get to have her and do this and the world can be ours. That's it, I guess. I feel like the world is one big adventure, and I can't wait to share it with her."

"That's so cool," a girl said. "I don't think a guy will ever talk about me that way."

"It'll happen," he said. "You'd be surprised. I certainly didn't think it would happen to me."

Jenna smiled and Ron searched her face. She had troubled eyes, somehow. Ron had said he could call her late into the night because she didn't sleep much. Maybe he thought he saw a way to fix her. He wanted to be the one to penetrate that 'weirdness' and shed light over her worry—soothe her somehow. But we should have known then that eighteen year-old girls never feel better—not until they turn twenty-one and can get into something different, or something.

I don't know. But she had a sweet smile, tentative like a shoot of new grass.

"My parents divorced when I was thirteen," she said.

"Are you glad they did?" I asked.

"I am now. I wasn't glad at the time, that's for sure. But kids never understand what's going on. I probably will never understand until I'm there myself."

"Hopefully you'll never be there yourself," I pointed out.

She shrugged.

"Did they fight a lot?" I asked.

"Not around me," she said. "It just sort of came as an announcement one day. In fact, I remember that my mom told my dad that she loved him that morning. It just seemed so unfair, so not right."

"Were you angry?"

She bit her lip, thinking back. "Yeah, I was angry. I wondered how they could do that to me—for a long time I always said I hated them."

"Did you?"

"No," she said. "I hated what had happened. I didn't hate them."

I nodded. "Do you find that their divorce affects you now in relationships?" I glanced at Ron, who winked at me.

"What do you mean?" she asked.

"Well, take you last boyfriend. When did you break up with him?"

"About four months ago."

"Okay," I said. "What was his name?"

She gave me a 'what the hell?' look and answered, "His name was John."

"How long did you and John see each other?"

"Well—going out actually lasted about three months but we were together for about a year."

"All right," I said. 'Why did you break up?"

She caught herself and smiled at a girl a few feet away with long brown hair who was listening. "Beverly knows about it," Jenna said, pointing to her. "She was there."

"But I asked you."

"Are you sure you want to hear the whole story?"

"Lay it on me," I said.

"Well, it was like this," she said, and considered a moment. "We had been seeing each other but things had sort of cooled down and I think he liked me a lot more than I liked him."

"Okay."

"Well, we were at this party and I did something that got him pretty mad."

"Which was?"

"I was making out with another boy."

I glanced at Ron. "Not your boyfriend?" I said.

"No," she said. "And he got pretty crazy and he actually hit me!"

The girl who had been there, Beverly, nodded that it was the truth.

"That's not cool," Ron said. "Did you hit him back?"

"No," she said. "I waited until he left, then we drove over to his house and smashed out all the windows in his car."

"He must have been a heavy sleeper," Ron observed.

"I guess so. Then later a friend of mine stole a bunch of CD's and some money out of his car. We sold the CD's and bought beer with the money."

"All right!" Ron said.

"You didn't keep any of the CDs?" I asked. "You know, souvenirs, or something?"

Beverly laughed. "They were all Christian music."

"There's some good Christian music out there," I said.

Please," Beverly drawled, and took a drink of her beer.

"Finish the wine cooler, Jenna," Ron said. "I'll finish this full beer before you finish your wine cooler. I bet you."

"Yeah, right," she said. She gulped the last of the cooler down while Ron struggled with the can of beer.

At some point in the night Ron and Jenna went away together and I found myself on the balcony with Beverly. We were both loose from the mixture of Coors and wine coolers and she had started yelling across the parking lot at the lit windows of the fraternity. The sky was clear and it was still warm—the streets welcomed all sorts of people. They walked around in small groups. Most of them were from the dorms on campus, looking at the doorways and windows of the slumping houses. A bright, wet Fall night in Eugene: the sky velvet-black and the water on the streets shining under the yellow lamps.

"Hey, boy—oys!" she yelled into the night. Someone shouted back at one point, asking something, I think, about a couple of frat members who had been here earlier, promising drinks to any girls who wanted to leave with them.

But she just laughed and stuck out her tongue when they squeaked open their sliding window.

"You want some of this?" she shouted, slapping her hip. "Well, you can't have it!" She laughed more and emptied her can of beer, tossed it into the air beyond the balcony where it sparkled as it fell and hit the ground clanking.

Through the windows I saw other groups of people inside. I didn't know any of them and I couldn't see Ron anywhere.

"Did you see where Jenna and Ron went?" I asked.

She looked at me, then pulled her chin back and said like a haughty popular kid: "Don't know—don't care." She flicked her hair for emphasis.

"Are you and Jenna not getting along or something?"

"Oh," she said. "She just all in there with her boy and leaves me all broken-hearted out here. She knows full-well that I just had a break-up and does she stick by her sister? Hell no."

"A break-up, huh? What happened?"

"What you need to do," she said, grabbing the balcony to steady herself. "Is find some more beer. Or us some more beer, if you would like to drink with me."

"You'll let me drink with you, huh?"

"Oh, sure. You seem like a fun guy. And in fact, I even remember your name. Ben. You—are—Ben." She emphasized the last three words and smiled to herself.

"Well, you—are—Beverly," I said. "That's not so hard."

"It is when you've drunk as much as I have," she declared. "Oh, now you're going to think I'm bad or something—well, I'd like it better if you think that." Beverly laughed. "Now get me some beer, Ben."

I shook my head and went inside, ducking through the hole in the door, and opened the fridge. I grabbed four cans and went back to the balcony, set all four of them on the railing then selected one and popped it for her, handed it over with flair.

She thanked me with a smile and nod, observing in a cheesy voice: "Well, aren't you such a gentleman!"

"In training," I said.

"I'll train you some more."

"Sure." I cracked the cold can and drank, felt my head swim as I pulled it forward from the long drink.

"Woah, man," she said. "You almost fell." She touched my shoulder to steady me, then pulled her hand away.

"I am so okay," I said. We stared at the frat house as she took a drink. I felt like a contest was starting. I was in a strange mood, felt it settling down my forehead like a hat too tight. The night was sharpened, filled with openings and slots to pole-position through like an Indy 500 driver.

I looked at her and her face sparkled, shined in the dark, her eyes shadowed and secretive. But her smile said 'come after me.' The fix of her chin, angle of her expression as she looked back at me pulled me toward her but I also knew that that I didn't care—didn't care much what she said. At that time I guess I was looking for someone, wanted to find someone who lit those feelings, that compulsion. This girl was here and the motivation and the now were edging her into focus, into target.

Finally, as she took another sip of her Coors and gave me a sweet and sour smile, curling her lips, crinkling her eyes, laughing in a fake self-conscious way at whatever I had said, the weird feeling clicked and I slid into the race, hot for those slots, ready to win through.

"So—your break-up," I said. "Tell me about it."

"Why should I tell you about it?"

"Because I'm listening."

"Any other reason?" she asked, eyebrows high. "Hmm?"

"Curiosity—I'm curious."

"And why are you curious?"

"Beverly!" I said. "You're talking but you're not saying anything. I'm curious about you. People don't have reasons for being curious. They just are. So what I do is ask questions and then I figure out why it was I wanted to know whatever I wanted to know."

She pouted. "And what did you want to know, Ben?"

"What was you're ex-boyfriend's name?"

"His name was Blake."

"Okay. What did he do?"

"He sold drugs."

"Really? That's interesting. What sort of drugs did he sell? Are you saying he was a pharmacist? Did he work in a pharmacy?"

"No," she said dryly. "He didn't let me know what he sold. He didn't want me in on that sort of stuff. I was just around whenever he wanted somebody to fuck on."

"That's a nice way to put it," I said.

"Well," she corrected, "he did say he loved me and I think in a way he did. But he said he had appearances to keep up."

"He had appearances to keep up?"

"Yeah, you know—the player, the lady's man. His friends were real important to him and they seemed to think having me around was a bad idea. So…away went Beverly."

"He sounds a little shallow."

"Well, that's what was important to him. His friends and his drugs."

"Did he do a lot of drugs?"

She shrugged. "Crystal meth was what he was on most of the time. I guess he was addicted to it or something—a tweaker. He never stopped talking about menthol cigarettes and crystal meth, his two favorite things. Crystal Cool. Supposedly he's clean now. All he does is smoke pot but that's all right with me."

"Did you ever have a moment with him when he wasn't on something?"

Beverly cocked her head and grinned, pushed at the air between us with a limp hand. "You're trying to be some kind of psychiatrist with me or something," she accused.

"Never," I said. "I'm just curious."

"Sure, yeah," she said, and looked at the frat house. Suddenly it was so obvious that she didn't belong with these types of people. She seemed too Springfield, trying too hard to be something else. Suddenly she seemed entirely different than when I had first begun talking to her. I thought she looked scared, nearly. The finger tracing the rim of her beer can made her mordant, tragic among these rich kids. I could see that she had wanted this Blake to mean something. Or she wanted everything to mean something—

"How did you meet Jenna?" I asked.

"We have some classes together at L.C.C., and we worked together for a while. That's how I know about her ex-boyfriend."

"Really?" I said, taking another beer, popping it and passing the can into her loose grip. Then I gave her a smile. "Was it you who stole the CDs and money out of his car?"

She blustered and sprayed her drink all over the railing. Beverly held her hand to her mouth as she reeled, laughing. "How'd you tell that?" she demanded.

"Just a guess."

"Well, don't tell anyone."

"Why did you do it? Did you know the guy too?"

"See, I didn't tell you where we worked because I was a little embarrassed about it."

"Don't be embarrassed."

"We worked at McDonald's—and the guy, Jenna's ex, was our shift manager. Oh, he was a cock! I loved the look on his face when he said his car was broken into. Poor baby, all his stupid Christian CDs were gone. Ha!" She chuckled, eyes sideways as she remembered.

"You didn't have something going on with this guy, too, did you?"

"Me? Oh, no. Nothing big. He grabbed my ass once but I didn't do anything about it. I didn't even tell Jenna because I knew she was head-over for him. I'm down with the sister rule and all—I'm not about the step to another girl's man."

"Well, he had a great job," I said. "I bet he was a real catch."

"You shut up! You said you wouldn't tease me."

"I'm sorry," I said sheepishly. "Do you forgive me?"

"No," she said.

"But—back to Blake. You got us off the track. How did you break up?"

"I told him to kiss my ass and left his house."

"Did he try to get you back?"

"Oh, he still calls me every now and then. But I never return his calls. I see what a loser he is now."

"But he loved you didn't he?"

"Maybe, but I don't think he knew what love was."

I leaned forward, half-smiling.

"What is love, Beverly?" I asked.

"Oh, jeez!" she shouted. "There you go being all serious and asking serious questions. Are you trying to hit on me, Ben?"

"Curiosity. Tell me."

She stared at me, eyes wide in the dark, the glint of her silver beer can reflected in her shiny irises. Then she smiled and turned to the fraternity windows and catcalled, "Love is, Psi Chi! Love is—is—is!"

Beverly turned back toward me and composed her grin into an interview-serious expression. "Well, Ben," she said like a news anchor. "To me—To me love is beautiful. Love is the ultimate. Love is the total rush, the complete happiness. It makes you all fluttery inside and makes you blab on for hours. I don't know any better feeling."

"Have you felt it a lot?"

"A few times. Sometimes I didn't know what I was feeling until it hit me later: that the anxiety attack was love grabbing me. Sometimes I didn't even know until it was over and the guy was jerking me around like they all do. Then I just felt hurt because I didn't even know what was going on and suddenly it's over. You know what they say, 'Girls fall first, guys fall harder.' Well, I always fall first. I always put my stupid neck out and get it chopped off. But that's what it's all about. It's good even when it's bad."

She sighed. "I mean, that's why it's so cool to hear somebody like that engaged guy who was here earlier—because he's there and he knows and, I mean, what can be better than that?"

"There's nothing better than that," I said. "There really is nothing better."

"Ooh," she said. "Ben's romantic! Well, what do you think love is serious-boy?"

"Me? I don't know. I honestly don't."

"You've got to. Haven't you ever liked anybody?"

"Nobody but you."

"Now you're talking out your ass, boy. You better stop." Her eyes sparkled hotly. "Come on. Tell me!"

"Sure," I said, shrugging. "I guess I've liked people, whatever that means."

"Well, how do you know when you like them then, if you don't know what it means?"

"Fine," I acquiesced, glancing around. "Um—If I can't get her out of my mind. If I get all 'fluttery' like you said. My big thing is rehearsing what I'll say to someone, or walk around worrying over what I could have said. I'm always making conversations in my head between me and girls I've met, scenarios and whatnot."

"Fantasizing, you mean?"

"I guess, yeah. Fantasizing all the time, that I guess people even say my lips move while I'm doing it."

"And what do you imagine in these scenarios? Sex?"

I smiled. "Not always. But it usually ends in that, yeah. No, I think about lots of things. Dinner conversations, walks, talking about classes, what she might think of something in a class, what she thinks about life. Anything. I don't know."

"And do you ever talk to these girls or do you just make up these conversations and then beat off?"

"No! I talk to them. I'm talking to you aren't I?"

"You're only talking to me because I haven't passed out yet and there's nobody else around," she said.

"That's not true."

"Sure it is. It's called 'Last Call Syndrome.'"

I grinned. "Why, does this sort of thing happen to you a lot?"

"Not where I let it go on so long usually…No, I'm not a last call type of woman."

"Oh, and what sort of woman are you?"

"I'm a bitch, that's what. You'd better look out for me."

"I'll be sure and do that." I finished the last of my beer and there was quiet for a second as she watched me. Then she faced the railing again, leaning over, and swung her legs behind her.

"Yeah," she said. "I thought that was pretty cool what that guy said about his fiance. You never seem to hear stuff like that any more." She laughed. "He was probably full of shit. She's probably a stripper or something."

"Hey, there are plenty of honorable strippers."

"Whatever," she said.

"Are your parents still married?" I asked.

"Yep. Almost twenty-four years now. Sometimes I don't know how they stand each other but they've stuck it out. Are yours?"

"No," I said slowly. "They divorced in July. They were married twenty-eight years."

She looked at me. "Oh, I'm sorry. That must have been hard. Did you know it was coming?"

I turned and leaned my chest against the railing, close enough to her that our shoulders touched. The bare skin of her arm pressed against my elbow. She was warm and peach-scented.

I breathed deep of the cold night air, felt it lick at the fuzz in my head. I searched the parking lot but there was nothing between us and the frat house. Beverly's thrown beer can flickered silver on the asphalt.

"I knew things weren't great, I guess. But I didn't expect the divorce or anything. It was real quiet the whole time, as long as I can remember. I think it was lots of little things finally—I don't know." I lifted my heavy head and peered at the sky, the blue space and gauzy clouds across the September moon.

"You spend your whole life thinking this is the way things are," I said, "and when suddenly you find out that what you know is wrong, that your whole foundation is wrong, it ruins everything. I mean, my mom used to say thing like, 'I love your father but I'm not in love with him' and I would just think 'okay.' I think as the kid you just hear this things and you see the fact that every time your dad tries to hug your mom she pushes him away, but you don't believe those things. You think that's how it's supposed to be. I haven't been in other people's houses. I don't know how they live—so what else do you know? That's how it is. That's how it works. This is what you'll get someday. And when my brother left the house all of a sudden that picture started to change, you know? Things weren't so glued together and the pieces started to fall apart."

"Where'd your brother go?" she asked.

"Portland first. Now I don't know where. We haven't heard from him in a year."

Her expression sobered a little and she touched my hand. "Were you close to your brother?"

"Uh—I really looked up to him. That's one of the things that gets me is that I don't think I knew him as well as I could have. I wish he could know me now. I wish I could have known him. Not knowing what's happening with him, or why he wouldn't want to talk to *me* at least, that makes it worse. It makes me think a lot. But it doesn't do too much good worrying about it all the time."

"Sometimes it's good to talk about it." Beverly punched my arm lightly. "Huh, curious-boy?"

I smiled and pushed her back. "Yeah."

"Do you know why he did it?" she asked. "Did he send you a letter or anything?" Then she caught herself. "If I'm getting too personal or anything, let me know."

"Nah." I shrugged, letting her know it was okay. Her warm arm soothed me where we touched. "He didn't say anything."

Beverly nodded.

"A lot of the time it was like I didn't exist," I said. "Once Garret was gone they didn't bother trying anymore. He's still the only thing my mom can talk about when I go home."

"You're existing right here with me," she said. "I'm pretty sure."

Then she pushed herself away from the railing and spun a circle with her arms wide.

"What we need now," Beverly said, "is a change of subject."

This girl was okay.

"And more beer," I said.

"Maybe. Is the music still playing inside?"

"I don't know. I think most everybody's sacked out except for us."

"Oh, that's okay," she said, waving a hand. "They're all drunk. They'll sleep like rocks. I want to listen to some musique-a on the stere-o. Let's go, Benjamin."

"More beer," I suggested, following her through the hole in the screen door.

"You'll have to look," she said. "I think we might have had the last of it. Where'd you find what we just drank?"

"In the fridge. It was hidden in the salad cooler—but there was lots of it."

"Well, search it out, man! But if everybody drank what's in there, don't worry. I've got my own secret stash of the hard stuff."

"The hard stuff, huh? How old are you?"

I'm twenty years old. How old are you?"

"I—" I said, pointing at my chest, "am nineteen years-old. I'm still a teenager, which is less than you can say."

She laughed. "And are you still a virgin, little Ben?"

"That's for me to know and you to find out."

"You want me to find out, huh?"

"I want you to take me to the hard stuff because this fridgerator is totally empty."

"Empty?" she repeated.

"Entirely, and there was a lot in here when I got our beer."

"Well," she said. "Come with me."

Beverly led me down a dim hallway to her room. Some people were crashed in the living room and soft noises came from a closed door as we passed. She glanced back at me and smiled at the sound.

Then she took my hand.

"Be vehwy, vehwy quiet," she whispered, and I laughed silently.

The alcohol buzzing in my head made the dark grainy and thick—like the black space in an overexposed photo. The grains in the dark held steady and then lurched like germs under a microscope, crawling, oozing. They paused before hopping again with the thump of my heartbeat.

She creaked open the door to her room and kicked some clothes out of the way, closed the door carefully behind us then moved to a corner and lit a squat blue candle. The flame wavered against the heavy dark, then threw orange light up the wall behind it, revealing her futon and a Jim Morrison poster on the wall. His brooding eyes glared out from wells of black. She tapped a button on her stereo and 'Being Boring' by the Pet Shop Boys floated across the floor.

Then she sat cross legged in front of the futon and showed me a flask that had appeared in her hands. She unscrewed the silver cap and tipped it to her lips, made a squeezed face and passed me the flask.

I sat facing her, holding the warm flask. "What is this?" I asked.

"Liquid acid," she said, smiling. "Try it."

"I won't go schizo, will I?" I asked.

She stared at me, then giggled. "That's—What is that?"

"Animal House," I answered. "Filmed on the U of Oregon campus not two blocks from right here."

"I knew that. I love that part."

I tipped the flask and felt the warm glow of whiskey hit my tongue. I choked a shot down and then steadied myself as the room tilted.

"Beer then liquor, never sicker," Beverly said. "What do you think?"

"Well, it's definitely the hard stuff. I don't think I'm going to be able to drive home now."

She laughed. "You were planning on it?"

"I had plans, you know, in the back of my mind and places—" I waved a hand as the thoughts flickered in my head. "Plans for stuff."

"What kind of stuff?" she asked.

"I think," I said. "I forget." I looked around slowly at the walls lit by the swaying candlelight. "So this is your room, huh?"

"This is it. Do you like it?"

"Jim there kind of scares me," I said, pointing to the poster. "But everything else seems right as rain. Looks like a college kid's room ought to look. By the manual. By the book. You know."

How many bedrooms like this, how many pockets of personality in the university's periphery, futons, posters, candles, used textbooks, tape decks, lamps shaded by paisley cloth?

"Sure," she agreed. Beverly set her hands on her knees and leaned forward slightly. The candle warmed the planes of her face to a gold glow, soft curves fuzzed into shadows from her hair—a painting in watercolor blurred by my staggering vision. But she had great brown hair, like chocolate: deep, rich, and suddenly I ached to run my hands through it, ached to melt into the soothing curves of her skin, her lips.

Her room smelled of peach lotion. The carpet was rough to my flat hands as I held myself up.

She smiled then—seemed to search through my eyes as though my thoughts listed like lines on a teleprompter across them—and tilted her head, tucked her hair behind an ear and revealed even more of her glowing face.

"Ben," she whispered. "Do you do this all the time?"

I half-frowned. "Do what all the time?"

"Seduce unsuspecting girls like this?"

"I've seduced you, huh?" I said.

"Well, you remember what I said about girls falling first?"

"And guys falling harder. Yeah. What did you mean by that?"

Beverly kissed me. She put a hand on the back of my neck and pulled me closer. And it wasn't much farther to the floor, where she twined her legs in mine, kicking her shoes off.

"You've got to watch me when I get drunk, Ben," she warned. "I can't control myself."

The whiskey really hit after that. The world rolled and tumbled and unfortunately I don't remember a lot of the rest of the night. I regret that.

Driving Under the Influence

Anger. Broiling sweaty stoplight anger. And honey, let go of the wheel. Honey don't hit me like that. Honey, please.

Throw yourself away from me into the corner of the seat and the door and press your cheek on the cold glass while the street lights slide off the black windows into your eyes and disappear, lost in those shadows. The lights gliding by serene as outer space. Baby, don't scream like that. Honey, let go of the wheel.

Look out.

We're swerving all over the road.

I forgot about the lights rounded in your tears: wipe them away. There, it's okay. But I won't touch you if you don't want me to. Hands tight on the wheel. Please, don't yell like that. Just let me relax. It's been a hard day and all I would like is to unwind a little without the yelling. Don't hit me now.

Honey, let go of the wheel.

So the rear slips a little right and quick turn with a spray of gravel leaves us halted on the shoulder in the black beneath the trees. Abruptly the radio finds volume; the car hums. I move one hand to quiet the radio down. Look at you there.

Words like weights, slow to lift.

"If you want to get it done," I say, "we'll get it done."

Your eyes are like black diamonds in the dark, glimmering. And without meaning to my eyes slip down to the seat belt and your stomach against it; lower center of gravity than mine. You sit differently, hips thrust forward. That slim nylon against your middle, half shiny in the shadows.

Accusing eyes. You protect your stomach from me with spread hands.

Explosions again and words slam the ceiling like bombs, shatter on the windshield, nail through me when I feel each burst of your breath, every enunciation you power from your middle.

Stare at me, breathing.

I say, "I don't know if I want to get it done," but that seems even worse. You start to cry because you feel so alone with no one to help you, no one to lean on.

Ah, you turn away again and of course there's no way I can help. Nothing I can do. You're right, of course. My touch is disgusting. My face repugnant. I am the root of your unhappiness.

I feel it welling there: that vast carelessness that hits me at times like these. Probably the worst times but it makes me feel better anyway.

And I know you're there and miserable but suddenly I just don't care much anymore. Something from my father; some male gift of protective indifference. Some ability to take what I know is real, important and necessary and shove it a thousand miles away to the farthest corner of my consciousness. Push you away. There. Like that.

"Fine," I declare, and release a long breath.

Car in gear: shove that gas pedal.

Radio up a lot louder than before.

You're a part of the sliding scenery. All your worries of work and money and classes melt into a yellow line drawn by the headlights, and I run it over.

There was the mall today, full of sunshine and tall green plants leaning like women at gossip all along the walls. And the girls too, a striped cotton parade of spaghetti-strapped tank tops and pony tails, sunbleached, swinging side to side. What are they doing there? Catalog models out for kicks on these hot summer days. Finding their souls here, when the high school boys who must be their own ages gawk from a thousand innocences away, sucking on straws. But those girls lower their butterfly wing sunglasses to release just a glimmer of those opal eyes like oil boiling in the sun (*snap, snap*) plus atom bomb smiles with unnaturally white teeth sparkling. Aim all that right at those poor young boys and you wonder what fantasies they fuel, forever unattainable. Because she found me with a flicker of her gaze, flashing black eyes—never completing contact. Strode right by with her tight shirt as conversation; ass-tight jeans with that flat spot between her legs to let the sunshine through, shaped vaguely like a key hole, round with sloping sides.

Glance at the blushing boys. But I know what that flat spot's for.

She smiled.

Flashing slide show of breasts and asses, almond-shaped eyes and curved lashes, chestnut, blonde, burning scarlet and ultra-black splashes of hair on warm butterscotch shoulders.

"I know you're here, you don't have to shout," I answer. Scowl at me from the corner of the seat and the window, arms crossed over your chest.

I've always thought you had a great chest. I don't know if I ever said it. And ass, too: great ass.

Jesus.

Let go of the wheel. I'm tired of this, honey. Mary, I'm serious. Let go of the goddamned—

"*Fuck! Are you even listening to me?*"

Please don't make me yell. But you've done it. Somehow you've penetrated the carelessness. Reached your claws inside to swirl me around.

But I still don't care. Don't you see? I'm just mad now because you won't leave me alone. It was such a nice silence. Almost able to forget for a moment.

Yes, I care! Yes, I give a damn! But what am I supposed to do here, huh? What am I supposed to say that won't be the wrong answer? Say what I want? Oh, well isn't that a merry load of—

Let go of the wheel.

Let go—

But there it is: the blossom of sparkling white and crimson lights in the rearview, cool needles in the base of my skull, straightening my spine. Eyes rapt on the rotating flower of fire against the black. And fear, chilly across my forehead.

"Oh, great."

My license and registration are sitting on the hood of the car. I can see you watching me through the windshield; until you catch my eyes and turn your head away.

"Why don't you hold up your hands, son," says the state tropper. He's in his sixties at least.

I raise my hands and he frowns.

"Not like that," he says. His voice is low. "Chest level."

He drops the flashlight's beam from my face and sniffs the tops of my hands briefly.

"You don't smell like alcohol, son," he says. He shines the light directly in my eyes and I blink. "You taken any drugs tonight?"

"No, sir."

He grunts. "Then why were you driving like a maniac?"

"We were having an argument," I say.

But a passing car flings my words away.

"What's that?" he says. "Speak up."

"I said we were having an argument."

"That must have been some argument."

I don't know why I tell him. "My girlfriend is pregnant. We don't know what to do about it."

"Do about it?"

"Whether she should get an abortion or not."

"I see." The trooper glances at you in the car a second before moving his eyes to look at me, squinting in the dark.

"Why don't you come over here," he says.

I follow him about twenty feet away from the car. The headlights from his patrol car send a fan of light across the road, over our car and I can see the silhouette of your head against the windows, the rhythmic flashing of red and blue on your hair. I have my back to the light but his face is illuminated, pale and finely wrinkled, crows feet and silver-gray eyebrows. Eyes watching me. Thumbs hooked in the tooled leather belt that holds his pistol and nightstick, his handcuffs. Polyester shirt rounded by his belly. We both shift colors with the flashing lights.

"Hold your arms out," he says. "Touch your nose."

As I'm doing it, he says: "I've been married thirty-two years, son. I got married because my girlfriend was pregnant. Not long after that she became my wife. That's what you did back then."

"We're both college students," I say.

"All right." He backs away from me ten feet. My shadow ends at his shoes. "I want you to walk towards me, putting one foot right in front of the other."

"I never made it into college," he tells me. "Whether that's because Julia got pregnant, I can't really say. I don't think I would have made it anyway."

I stop a few feet in front of him.

"All right," he says. "Cross your arms, and I want you to balance on one foot."

"Well, son," he continues. "I'm not going to give you any answers. I got married when I was twenty-one. Between you and me, I haven't been the most faithful husband, and I can't say I love my wife. But I'm fifty-three years old and I've got three children and two little grandkids, and at this point I can't say it matters too much. Go ahead and relax."

I drop my foot to the ground and stand looking at him. The blue light pulses cool, the red comes like a punch.

"I don't mean to be rude," I say. "But that doesn't really help me at all."

He smiles. "One thing I've learned is don't ever say you don't mean to be rude, because you always do. You'll just piss people off even more. And I wasn't trying to help. I'm just letting you know how it is."

He tips his hat. "I suggest you sit here for a while and figure out your problem before you do anymore driving. You have a good night now, son."

Then he goes back to his patrol car, his face whitening as he walks into the light, until he's past me and in a second switches off the flashing lights.

I look back toward the car and I see you there, your turned face lit by the headlights. You're watching me.

Seventh Beer Thoughts

A glowing globe of light around the street lamp: bugs boiling under the moon. This pacing has to be the worst thing. Because he had some decisiveness earlier when he and Jon were sitting drinking and he realized he had to have his books back.

They were important books or had been at one point and it didn't seem right to have to go buy new ones. Especially when it should have been easy to ask for them back. But that would have meant talking to her and right now that was out of the question. Out of his head anyway after seven beers. That was just enough.

They had grown up in this town and had never been in the bar. It was called the Wagon Wheel and down behind the Ford dealership downtown. Jon had said, "What the hell? We're men aren't we?"

That had clinched it and Mike winked as he pulled the heavy door open to the black interior—adventure crouched beyond, right under their noses all this time. The two of them thinking Eugene bars were what it was all about. And right here in Cottage Grove sat a great place to drink pitchers of Michelob only $4 each. That was a deal. The bar reminded him of some bar in a book: *Fat City* by Gardner, the guy who hadn't seemed to have written anything else after that one fantastic book about amateur boxing in a shit hole town called Stockton. Maybe Stockton was bigger but it had Cottage Grove's soul. They decided that was true.

The problem was that she had the book. Rather, Mike had left it at her place. That was where this magnificent plan hatched. Break into her house and get the book. Hadn't he done it a million times, creeping through the back door to crawl into bed with her, brushing his lips against the warm nape of her neck? The books were in a box under the desk in her room and what could be easier than getting in there, when she didn't even sleep in that room? She said it was too cold.

Up there, the boiling bugs. At the end of the block sat the house, black under the big walnut trees her father grew from black walnuts brought from Missouri, rolling around in the bed of his pickup all the way. When he used to haul-ass all night just to see her mother. What a man, commanding the dinner table with a cigarette cradled between fat fingers.

Down the street and up the street from inky dark into the yellow pool beneath the street lamp. No lights on. The trouble was, he knew exactly where she was in the house, could pinpoint the exact side of the bed, the exact lilt of her cheek against the pillow, and suddenly it didn't seem so great being alone in the world with the sky rotating overhead on an ice-cold night like right now.

Where had Jon gone? It had been his idea, hadn't it? No, no. He had to work. Jon had a job. Jon didn't have an English degree and pending student loan payments and a lifestyle that hadn't yet slipped into working. You know, working. What he had done in high school. What Jon had been doing this whole time. Whenever the girls at the parties said, "What classes are you taking?" and Jon got to say—novel stuff—"Well, I'm working." Productive working.

And they would invariably say: "That's so cool. You know, that's so cool you're doing that. I totally respect you. This shit I'm doing—I don't know why I'm doing it half the time, you know? But that's so cool You're doing something."

Nodding Jon, the totally respected forklift operator, wheeling that crazy cart backwards on its third wheel all over the warehouse yelling,

"Mike, check this out!" Hunched over the wheel like an old man in an Oldsmobile. Because work was easy for a working stiff like him. But for a kid who could rap all day long on post-modernism and its evolution from Elliot to DeLillo, work just wasn't something so easy. Not when all those slimy retail executives looked at English and smarmed out, "Oh, no Business degree, huh?" That's what it's all about: bugs, boiling bugs. Talking about the business necessary to afford even a $4 pitcher of beer.

On his bed at home were spread all sorts of brochures for cruise ship jobs: "See the World and Make Some Great Money!" above the smiling busboy and girl. This of course was all a symptom of Sheryl. Cruise ships and night rants just wouldn't be right without the added bonus of standing in a parking lot watching her drive away, yelling at tail lights with all the faces spinning like turrets in a guy's direction while he just screams at a receding vehicle that he loves her.

And when he falls on the pavement, dropping his head on a parking curb, isn't that something worth watching in detail? Especially that guy in the VW van. That guy stood out especially. The guy with the purple beret. "Dude, you need a hit, man?" that guy asked. So Mike could lift his head from this stone pillow and say, thanks man, no thanks.

"Rock on, brother," said purple beret guy. This Mike feels, summarizes his college career. And back in Cottage Grove these events are disjointed and but significant, somehow. In the same way that his best friend Jon recognizes the relative importance and equal uselessness of the concept of post-modernism, and more importantly and equally useless, Mike's purchase of that knowledge in thousand dollar chunks.

Jon learned to drive a forklift for free and tonight he paid for the beer. As on many other nights. Even when two years ago a girl said, "What the hell is post-modernism, anyway?" at that same party and he was able to answer her in a corner, leaning forward to catch the warm periphery of her perfume.

Because that girl later turned magically into his Sheryl does not validate the importance or usefulness of that information. All this means is that he now has these images floating in his brain like coffee cups cruising blue skies (a professor's favorite metaphor). All that money. All that money that he really has no concept of yet: it was all payment for a feeling that came to him in the corner of that room with a mason jar of cheap wine in one hand and the other free to reach out and trace her cheek in an impulsive instant.

Where she smiled, and the tip of his finger was suddenly running the ridge of a dimple and this had to be serendipity, this gesture that somehow had worked. What did any of it matter? This is what mattered. It worked. These events aligned in the cosmic disregard that had until now been navigator for his soul. Suddenly now so many misunderstood events gained meaning—readiness for now.

Her eyes aquamarine shimmering scuba depths in cruise ship commercials.

That girl who would hold his hand and take charge of him in her best friend's dorm room. That same girl who said she didn't know what she felt anymore and, when he prompted like a fool, answered, "No, Mike. I don't know if I love you anymore."

This is the pain love is made of. To look around, look around at the staring faces in passing cars swiveling just like gun turrets. Even the homeless guy twenty feet away jiving to himself with the bottle in one limp hand didn't know that the hell was going on. A guy can only whimper, "Please," so many times and then this is where he finds himself, Mike, now, forehead on a cold hard lamp pole.

These girls. You know these girls. He wished he had some way to excise his memory because he knew that without the addition of her everything would be satisfyingly bland, four years of uneventful binge drinking and next term to look forward to until there were no more new terms. She made impending loan payments worthwhile. She kept him out of shit hole bars populated by the type of people he used to make fun of. She kept him away from the high school.

These kids, shouting things like, "I fucked a high school girl, Sheryl! Out at the lake! Last week!" Though slipping inside some sloppy seventeen year-old wasn't what he had thought. His dick felt like the handle of a toilet plunger inside this little girl shivering beneath him, eyes clenched shut. If he shouted her name a thousand times at the blank dark wall of her house would the lights come on? Would her dad yell at him and call the police like three nights ago? Hadn't she asked him once if he would fight for her? Hadn't she?

Boiling bugs. Going crazy up there in the ball of light, never going anywhere but up and down and around and back and forth, wild white wings flashing, whirring. He can barely hear them screaming up there at the burning light. Spermazoa at the egg. Should it let them in?

Here we go, slower now through the chain-link gate and around the back between the big laurel tree and the dark side of the house where the shadows drape like black velvet. Here comes the back door. Here it is. But look at that, they put a lock on it. They put a lock on it. Locked out of her life, Mike. You don't belong here anymore. Even though her dad said you seemed to have a level head on your shoulders. You know seem to know a few things, Mike. Tell me this—

Why can't he come in? Sheryl, it was only two weeks ago that you and Mike decided to separate for a while to "sort out thoughts." Are they sorted yet? Have you figured out what you're feeling? Oh, baby, don't do this anymore. He's dying. He's wilting inside, rotten, so busted up. Can't you see?

Turn around, back to the wall, sliding down because here's Shots the family dog licking his hands. Shots understands what love is, doesn't he? He can sense these feelings, a wet nose the true meter of sincerity.

How much? she said.

I would die for you, he said.

Silly.

I would die for you.

That's easy. Would you fight for me?

Yes.

No, really. When everything seems impossible and you'll never win, would you still fight for me?

Yes.

This from the girl who thought stalking was romantic. This from the girl who said go with your heart, Mike. Trust your heart, Mike.

"Sheryl!"

Stand-up, grab that screen door. Crazy Shots, barking like a demon. Locks are nothing.

"Sheryl!"

Silly door.

"Sheryl, I want my books!"

That old man's yelling again.

Wild Duck: Eugene, Oregon

She moved here from California. This is what the long wheat-blonde hair says. When she gives a quizzical smile and asks, "How did you know?" it has to be the fourth or fifth time a guy hears those words if he's from around here and spends a lot of time at the Wild Duck on a given Saturday night. It might have been Doc's Pad or Joggers or possibly the Vet's Club. It's all the same.

What a guy should enjoy in particular is the glitter on her cheeks. That's fresh out of high school or damn close and that makes her special indeed.

This guy might have been the first one to take an interest in her since she moved here. Surely, she hasn't told anybody else about her father and mother and her little sister, Bobby. Not a guy, anyway. She describes these concepts too eagerly. She doesn't glance around like a lot of the girls. She hunches down, holding her drink in two hands and grins at this special guy in front of her who just revealed a secret she was aching to tell somebody.

Par for the course, she has a lot of convictions about sustained farming practices and vegetarianism and youth hostels. A guy may or may not know about these things already. Listen regardless. The glitter is slightly fascinating after three drinks and its not a long walk home. She has things to keep talking about. She studied creative writing in New Mexico and then pottery on a reservation. She trusts people too much and a guy took advantage of her recently, stranding her in Portland.

"Maybe you shouldn't tell people that," a guy will suggest.

"Oh," she says, shrugging loosely. "I can't help it."

Accept this. The nice, regular guy will then comfort her with details from his own unremarkable life. He puts up with people at a photo booth in a discount retail store all day long. He rides a bike and gets splashed with mud all the time. She'll laugh and hang her blue eyes on a guy's face in response to tenderness like that.

He wishes he could be a photographer, a guy might tell her. But school. We all know how school is.

She'll touch a guy's hand and say she knows he'll make it someday.

Now is a good time to ask: "What's your name?"

And she'll smile and put one of her long hands on her cheek, watching the guy in front of her. She's had a few drinks too.

"Andrea," she'll answer. "And yours?"

A guy could say anything if he wanted but this guy tells her, "Mark. I'm Mark."

"Prove it," she says.

A guy can get smiley now. "What?" he could say. "You want my drivers license?"

"No," she says, lowering her eyes and watching him hard. "Tell me something that makes you Mark."

"Makes me Mark?"

"Something that when I hear it I'll think, only a Mark could do that. You know what I mean? Something only a Mark would think of."

A guy should have answers on hand for little games like this, he gets them so often. But this guy hasn't studied up and now all he can do is lean back in the booth, crossing his arms, studying the ceiling where beer posters swing.

"Okay," he says. The guy then leans forward with a sly smile and explains, "When I was fifteen I loved archery. I had a hay bail on saw horses in the back yard with a target on it. I practiced a lot. I mean everyday I came home from school and shot at that target. Plus, I was saving up for a compound bow."

Here he clears his throat. "Anyway, I practiced all through the winter, and the rain started eating the hay bail pretty bad, and it started falling apart, right? Well, I finally got enough money for a compound bow, and I went out and bought a compound bow with a 75 pound pull. That day, I went out and leveled the first arrow on the target, right? I let go, and the arrow hit the target dead in the center, but the hay bail was too rotten, and the bigger bow sent the arrow right through the hay bail into the side of our neighbor's motor home."

Here the girl will cover her mouth, grinning.

Here the guy will nod in slight embarrassment. "Right. So I had to go talk to the old man and he was pretty pissed. But when we went to pull the arrow out of the side of his motor home, we saw that the arrow had hit in the dead center of the O in 'Road King.'"

"Yeah?" the girl says, clapping her hands.

"Yeah. And he looks at me and he kind of gives me this grudging smile, right? And he says, well, Mark, at least you hit the mark."

At this point a guy will pause for effect.

"And it wasn't so bad anymore, even though I had to fix the hole in his motor home and I couldn't shoot in the back yard any more until I bought a cork target. So that's my story. Good enough?"

"Perfect," she says. "Very Mark."

At this point a guy and a girl might get sick of yelling over all the brash music and the roar of people and the clacking billiards in the corner. They might finish their drinks in three solid gulps and following that, still light-headed, a guy might suggest a walk.

Sure, she'll be interested at this point. But outside, like most girls, she'll distrust the fact that she met him in a bar. She'll say, "I suppose you take all the girls for walks, huh?"

Unlike the earlier question, a guy knows this one by heart.

"Um, I really don't get out that often. I work a lot. And it's a pain in the ass on my bike."

"Why tonight?" she'll say, thinking of destiny.

At this point he'll shrug, answering, "Just felt like getting out. I was thirsty, you know?"

Outside where the night is cool and brisk on their cheeks, and a girl can see her chosen guy fully under the street lamp, and she becomes quite pleased with herself, and his voice acquires an added depth of sincerity it lacked when they were yelling at each other inside, the fact that she met him in a bar seems already ancient history and easily overlooked. They were just walking by.

She'll smile and answer, "I know."

Stereo

Here's what we do: John grabs five old spark plugs from his dad's shop and Gil gets hold of a hammer somewhere. We pile the spark plugs up in the alley behind McCoy's Pharmacy and Gil slams them with the hammer five or six times until the ceramic coating crumbles off. These he picks up and passes out to everybody. I got hold of some beer bottles from my brother's place: these I line up along the brick wall with about six feet between them.

So we line up and start flicking the bits of ceramic at the bottles. Use a sort of sideways slider, like you'd skip a rock on a pond, and if you hit the bottle right the damn thing just breaks apart. It's crazy. But John says it has something to do with harmonics between the glass and the ceramic.

Anyway, after some practice and the bottles are all used up, we pocket the pieces of tile and wait until dark comes around, skateboarding over by the Safeway. Around nine o'clock we figure it's dark enough and take off, walking up 16th, checking out cars along the way. The lowrider in question is farther up the hill, and we're talking about how this has more to do with vendetta than theft. There it is, emerald green and slammed to the street, tinted windows, low-profile tires. Any wannabe's dream rig. We all hate the fucker who rolls around in it.

There's a street lamp about fifty feet away. Some lights are on in the house. We take turns running by, winging the bits of ceramic at the window until Gil's snaps right and the passenger side window is suddenly full of sparkling cracks. One more tap and the glass falls away. Gil takes post a little up the street, John down. I lean inside to unlock the door and once that's done I sit inside quick and go to work at the stereo face, reaching up under the dash to get at the one nut locking it to the support brace. Done. I push the stereo out from the back and lay it on the seat with all the wires trailing behind. It's a nice set-up: Alpine CD. But he's lazy. There's a removable face and he should have taken that in with him. I pull out as many of the wires from the dash as I can, then I take the wire dikes and start cutting. Six wires.

"Rick?" I hear.

"Yeah."

"You got it, man?"

"Yeah. You wanna go for the amp?"

"Nah, man. Let's get outta here."

But I want the amp. He's got tens in the back so it's got to be something good. I set my knees on the pavement and start feeling around under the seat for the amplifier. There it is. I slide it over that slight hump in the floor board and take the wire cutters to the fat wires feeding into it. One of the wires won't cut all the way through so I start working it back and forth to break the copper.

"Rick!"

"What?"

"Door, man!"

I stick my head up and there it is, the front door opening. I'm on the side away from the house.

I toss the stereo out into the street behind me, aching at the scratched face, grab the amp in both hands and wrench it toward me. My knees are hurting on the pavement.

It's a warm night.

There it is: "What the fuck? What the fuck are you doing?"

There's a lot of wire beneath the seat. Instead of snapping the wire, I'm pulling out all the slack.

The door slams against my back.

My thighs are burning after a shock against the running board. I fall against the passenger seat. Now he's trying to stomp my ankles. He's got boots on. My left ankle grinds under the edge of his heel.

I hear: "Roth."

That's the fucker's name. I swivel my head in time to see John cracking the trucks of his board up against Roth's cheek bone. His neck makes a right angle.

I fumble my hands on the edge of the seat and push out from the door, land on my ass in the street. The amp falls on the pavement in front of me, shiny under the street lamp, pink wire hanging on.

I climb up, grabbing my board.

"Who's got the deck?" I shout.

"Here!"

My ankle's useless. But here we go: pick up the amp and jerk back, snapping the damn wire.

"Okay," I say. "We set?"

16th has a pretty good grade. I glance back at Roth lying in the street. I tuck the amp under my armpit like a book, like a kid on his way to school. We jet through Coiner Park. The running's mainly to kill adrenaline.

He'll be at school tomorrow, where it says: "No Weapon Zone."

That's one of our jokes.

At the Window

It's not hard. Nothing hard about it. Been around the house. Last night. Cased around a couple times and tested the window. Edged the screwdriver beneath the lock, moved it. Pressed an ear against the window and listened for them inside. Her lying beside him. Ran fingers along the revolver's butt just listening.

Nothing through the glass.

Sure.

Went over it all day long. Everything she'd said. Just like she said. The moon gazing down with a silver gaze on everything. The silver fence. Side of the house bright silver. Bright as day.

Black sky.

So here it goes: Glance left then right edging the screwdriver under the lock, twist, turn. It's open. Slide up the window and pull the curtains aside with one hand and one hand patting the revolver before taking the sill and heaving up and through to roll onto the carpet beneath the window inside. Silver moonlight spilling all into the room. Two forms silver on the bed.

Straighten up real tall.

Is she sleeping? Faking real good or she just can't hear. Doing fine. Just like she said. He's on the right with his white arm across his forehead so lift the revolver and draw-back click the hammer leveling it somewhere toward his jaw. Adjust up, down, right then left.

Breathe.

Crack crack crack.

Oh God she's screaming but she jumped up and has her hands on her forehead just screaming and screaming.

"What are you doing?" Shouted against her screaming. "Shut up! Shut up! What's wrong with you?"

But she won't quit. She won't shut up. My husband's dead. You killed my husband. You shot my husband. Who are you? What do you want? Why are you here? Oh, what did we do to you?

It's me.

Why are you here? Oh God he's dead. I can't believe you shot him. Who are you? Why did you do this?

"It's me!"

A dog barking. There's a dog barking and behind in the silver moon-glow lights are coming on. People wondering what all the noise is about. People calling the police.

Breathe.

You need to calm down. It was going to be cool. You said it was all going to be all right.

Who are you? Why are you doing this? Oh my God he's dead. I can't believe he's dead. Oh please don't hurt me.

Breathe.

You need to be quiet. Be quiet now!

Oh God. Oh God. Why are you doing this? Why did you do this to us?

She's doing this. She's really doing this. After everything. Everything she said and everything she did. The sheets are all black.

You said you loved me.

Oh, God.

It's me.

Oh, God.

Oh, crack crack.

Crack.

Empty.

And quiet. Back through the window and pull it closed. Find the dark places and slip into them. Running now. Running.

Through the back yards. Across the swinging bridge to River Road. Too bright with street lights. Onto that dirt road just past. Dark trees now. The dark where only kids drive to make out. Fumble the cloth to wipe down all over the pistol. Scissor legs working harder than they ever have.

You can push yourself to do things you never thought possible, she said. When you're in love.

Don't Wake

Attention, patrons. Heightened security measures are in effect at this airport.

A man and a woman sitting together waiting for her flight. Her blue carry-on in the seat between them. The man lowers his head. He spins his wedding ring on his finger.

Do not leave your baggage unattended.

Noisy: voices: pages for taxis, crowd rustle, a child's wail slices high above—people flow behind the man and woman. Faces flashing, sinking, turning forward. There are verdigris lizards in the iron partition separating the waiting area and main aisle.

Outside the display windows that reveal the runway, a window washer cleans in long ovals.

The woman checks her watch.

Do not accept packages or luggage from strangers.

Her face beside him, on the other edge of the sky blue bag, is fallen but expectant. Tired. The black crescents beneath her eyes, though she has tried with makeup to hide her condition. Her earth-brown hair makes the shadows on her face that give her away, make her look sunken in her business suit. But she is beautiful. Oh, God, is she young and beautiful but sad, and does this overcast of sadness in her make her more desirable?

She stands as the boarding announcement clamors into the waiting area. The security message is repeating itself in Spanish now. This is El Paso. The runway outside is bright gray and faded yellow under the sun.

She stands and sighs, lifts her shoulders in her suit, lets them fall. Holds her head up. Reaches out for the blue bag beside her. And as the bag rises so does he, the man beside her wearing the wedding ring she is not. Rises shakily, looking around and driving his hands deep in his pockets—useless if he can't help her somehow. Her posture obvious that she is with him, but here without his help.

He pulls his hands out and examines one open palm. The actions fill the space that good-byes would fill.

Because she doesn't see his hands, already having turned and begun to walk toward the growing clot of bodies and bags near the entry tunnel to the plane. She glances back briefly—in her eyes, what?—and is now part of the crowd, is lost through the doors. First her red jacket being covered by pressing travelers and then the brown flash of her hair, hidden by a sidestepping black coat. Vanished around the curve. Out of existence.

The man eases himself into a vacant chair near the line pushing forward, reaching with a blind hand and finding an arm rest to help him down. In front of him, regardless, the line jerks and rolls, heads searching. Outside the floor to ceiling windows the squeegee takes its slow turns, clearing the glass, trailing streaks of detergent rainbows.

He puts his face in his hands.

In English now: Increased security measures are in effect at this airport.

Reduced to my memories. No future. This is how to stop time. I wish now desperately that I had stood on that black chair and grabbed at something more of her. Some last view I could hold close now that she was limited in me.

I sat in the plastic chair and tried to remake her in the space beside me, feel out the shape of her absence against me. Or I should have stopped everything even in the car, stopped it months ago, stopped her and said to her—said to her: These are the things I feel. This is what I know. But I did not use those moments. I didn't break any link in the chain taking her away from me.

Because where was I? I was in an airport. I watched a silent family watch television, saying nothing alone together. Three hours since she left but where was I? I should have called her parents—but she wouldn't be home yet and that would be awkward. They liked me.

They loved me, I think. But that would be hard for them, if I called. Just to hear something of her. Just to get out of here somehow. Some excuse for momentum. Somewhere.

I forced myself to stand. I was sore but hadn't realized until now. The airport was empty. It was late. I looked up and down the terminal. There were more green lizards in the carpet stretching away. The roof and walls were rounded, as if I stood in the fluted throat of some vast sea shell—here in the heart of the desert. Some piece of the past.

Anna was returning to the sea. Back to where we met in San Diego. Back to everything before I imposed on her life in a bar six years ago.

Six years. They go so quick and yet I wanted, now, to give every moment the depth it deserved, standing here alone.

I had to move. I had to go.

Outside the air was warm and dry, the sky deep emerald with its white sparkles. The sky was a blue velvet jewelry case. Exhaust blew sweet against the doors. She's going back west. She never wanted to be here anyway no matter what she said.

How could this desert sea be the California she loved. As I walked I was aware of the empty space beside me. I knew and felt her absence, the lack of her voice and her step and my awareness of her right there, in the slot in reality right there against me. Only warm air there. She was on a plane. She took off west, up over the mountains, over our apartment, into the desert and the thin gray clouds there shrouding the pearl moon.

My ring was cool on my finger.

Motion now. I needed to cross the street to the parking garage, get in the car and join the traffic flowing away from the airport. I needed to join the mess on this Saturday night out there, put the radio on the dance station and watch the street lamps surface from the black.

Because, now, what I felt was not freedom and I did not want to think of myself as free from my marriage, even though Anna had just left me, had given up on me. She had said I was not worth living with. And to that how could I reply? Knowing she was purposely trying to hurt me. I played her game just to talk with her, just to hear her voice reacting against mine, or take that high road that led me here, to an empty car and her on a plane: that high road of uncaring and fatigue and supposed standing up for myself. But standing up for what, my right to not feel?

Because I was driving right now. I was on the freeway surrounded by other cars sliding through the night. But I was not there.

She is with me still there. Where I'm trapped in that long silent ride home from the hospital, with the knowledge that our baby was dead there between us, eight days after his birth. I am there. That is where and what I felt and I couldn't understand how she could be anywhere else, even now.

So Anna was on a plane back to the San Diego I took her away from. To stay with her parents in their big house and figure out what was happening, who she was, and who I was, even though I was here and that's a question even I could not answer. I am thirty years old and I could not tell her who I was. And she looked at me and she said, Then how can you know me? And I couldn't tell her that it was through her that I found me—it was up against her that I saw myself. But nothing is like that. Nothing like that can be expressed or explained during real time. There were just more words, mostly hers, and me spreading my hands or running from her, room to room, until eventually she stopped chasing me and this is where we ended, now, in our separate spaces in this life.

And now I was scared.

Knowing I had lost her did not make me feel free or reckless as I may have thought it would but only like a failure. My hands on the steering wheel were useless hands. The city floating by, its lights and neon, was just more open space to surround me, space without her to make it vibrant and real.

Early yet for this club: her favorite. He followed her here, his memory of her already, from the airport. She walked ahead of him across the concrete dance floor, its configurations of stars and beams of light. There she was waiting at the bar like so many other nights. Her smile as her eyes lay upon him coming closer, joining her there.

Blink and she is not there. There are other women with their drinks and men at their ears. There is music pounding and the bartender shoving the cash drawer home, issuing napkins and limes.

There are other women in tight black dresses with their black hair and black eyes, the way they lean against the bar sideways, turning their necks to look out over the club, one hand on the bar. He's seen these women his entire time in El Paso, ever since he came from Oregon. These women with hot eyes and tan breasts.

Music crashing. In these waves of sound the world is mute, actions silent. A silent film with this mad piano player accompanying. Faces lowering and rising against the light.

Drink. Because she has left him he feels a powerful desire to give himself away, too, to tie it up.

The music is a gorilla on drums. Hammering his chest. She liked to get drunk here and lose herself in the sound and crowd, the energy waving and spilling on the dance floor, sweating from the heat in the floor's center until the lights came up in the morning. And what could he do but follow her inside there where the energy and life were coruscating, this conflagration of motion and rising and exploding from the friction of bodies on bodies and glistening skin. The girls wringing out their hair, tossing it way back away from their wet necks and shoulders, bodies still following the lumpy beat. Smiling white teeth and dark bloody red lips. Legs, knees, hips, elbows—working. Eyes tight on each other, the couple. Us. Isn't this being alive, Anna?

Guards wander the area: Heightened security measures are in effect at this dance club. And on the speakers writhe men in leotards and women with feather boas leaving arcs of down floating around their heads.

The music makes all the motion soundless. The people are going up and down.

A drink. He was her chauffeur. Her protector. The one who brought her home safe after her explosion of self in sweat and dance. Without him how could she smile so brightly? How could her mascara run and her hair tangle and she still be safe in this strange city? Without him how could she dance as she was dancing, free and crazy as she liked to say: she felt so free out there in the flux of crowd energy, crowd life. Cigarette smoke wafting slowly upward through the hot light beams and turning stars. The turning stars.

Would you like a drink?

"What?"

This woman leaning toward him so he can smell her hair—her perfume?—and her lips are suddenly close to his ear, asking him, offering.

"Sure. A beer."

She smiles. Her lips move against his ear.

"You choose. Whatever you think is good."

The woman who left on the plane, her name was Anna Sharp. He was her husband, Dale. At this moment Dale is sitting at the bar in his wife's favorite club in El Paso, Texas, where they used to dance until 3 a.m., and another woman has offered to buy him a beer, seemingly unfazed by his lack of interest in choosing the beer—or maybe she sees it as flirtatious trust, her opportunity to impress him or judge him or just presume something about a person she approached in a speechless dance club, in a world of looks and no useless words. Except those murmured right up against the ear, and an approach like that needs some assumption anyway. We are the images of ourselves on the music backdrop.

But Dale is flaccid right now. His feeling is that of a blade of grass in deep currents and he has a sense of fate hammering him. Fool, though: God helps those who help themselves. Forsake me.

Or this woman will help him, turning from the bar with some Mexican cerveza in her hand. She has blood red finger nails, she has blood red lips.

She is like a rose at night, he tells himself, thanking her for the beer.

And I'm too kind. Deep currents.

But the beer tastes good. He lifts it again to his raw throat. The clock on the bar says it's been five hours since she left. Not home yet: nearly though. So what: will he call her and beg her back, waste air fare like that?

He wants to say that she wanted to go and he let her but it doesn't feel right yet. This is because her leaving was on Anna's terms and not his, and this makes him feel generally uneasy. She wanted to go and he let her. I was too weak to stop her.

"My name is Marit," the woman answers.

And he answers her: "My name is Dale."

"Are you in the Army?" This is the second question any woman will ask a man in El Paso in a bar, if his haircut doesn't make it blatant.

He looks at her, holding the beer and scratching his head with his free hand.

"No," he says. "I'm a writer."

A writer? She widens her eyes in a generous way.

Marit is younger than he is and somewhat whore-like in her tight black dress. This appeals to him, her freedom. She is the opposite of long-term desire. She will not meet his needs. But the crease between her breasts continues to open and close slightly as she leans in and then sways back, touching his wrist as she laughs.

He is making her laugh, saying something.

These are words. This is eye contact. This is a smile. This is how you talk to a woman who is not your wife using the same techniques that made Anna love you. You think.

Anna is on a plane, headed for her San Diego.

One more beer and Marit wants to dance. Dale was expansive and bought the second round of drinks: two shots of tequila; her call, not his. And on the floor, surrounded, he is aware of her body as she presses it up against him. There are probably people who would recognize him here, knowing Marit is not Anna. But Marit is really quite beautiful, it seems to Dale, and he wonders what in the world caused her to choose him and continue to lock her eyes into his in this fashion. When she moves away from him she holds his hand, their fingers entwined, and right now that feels like the most arousing thing he has felt in a long time. Her fingers are gently sweaty now, slick against his. Her hair glimmers under the lights.

A strobe light kicks on and he gets only every second frame of her as she moves in the music, her body surging toward him, hot against him.

He realizes he hasn't taken his wedding ring off—he kept it as a way to needle Anna, really; even after she had thrown hers at him and it fell beneath the crack in the floorboards, where it stayed—buried treasure—but Marit doesn't seem to care. She must have seen it. Even felt it on his finger.

But she smiles and dances and sways with no care for rings. And Dale suppresses his usual question, his normal reaction to any situation: to ask himself, where is this going? Where will this take me? What am I doing? Instead: ignoring the ring but leaving it there, to take it off now would be gutless. He had never taken it off before. Not since she put it on his finger.

Dare her with it and be honest. For once be honest and just lay it out. This is who I am. This is my ring. I think I am married.

But my son is dead.

If he could have he would have told her that. I am here because my son died. But I shouldn't blame Andy. I can't blame him.

No: I am here because I couldn't deal with the death of my son eight days after he was born and I slowly pushed my wife away in the year it's been since then and now she doesn't want to live with me anymore, which she told me, so I know, and so she is on a plane going back to the city where I met her and I am still here. Forging a direct chain of undeniably true events.

And by the way I lied: I am in the army. I'm a captain. I graduated college and had to pay back an ROTC scholarship and they assigned me to the Patriot Missile System and here I am. Yes, I was in the Gulf War. Yes, I shot down Scud missiles. And yes I hate my job and always have—or I don't know, really. It tears me up. But Anna didn't like it. I know that. That was reason enough for me to get out of the army but now all this has happened and she just left me tonight, yeah, I just dropped her off at the airport and watched her get on the plane and she didn't even say goodbye. That hurt. Anna was my wife, by the way, if I forgot to mention that.

I'm not boring you am I?

So in this sense loud music is good because Dale can keep his mouth shut and just give himself away to it—the crowd, the drinks, the music, the escape lurking in here, the self-obliteration—and not care about What Next. What next was on a plane for San Diego, up in the clouds or maybe just now touching down. And secretly, even here, he longs for her and wishes her a safe flight and that he could call and know that she has arrived safely. But caring is no longer his luxury.

And the strobe has ended its dissection of time and Marit is flowing up against him again in long curves. She is looking at him and has pulled her dress down over her shoulders—apparently it stretches like that. Her skin is tan and her hair black.

Drinks, more drinks. She insists on buying: more shots. Dale feels his toes on the edge. At the bar his fingers play at his wedding ring and finally it comes free of his finger where it has been so long. His skin is worm-like where it rested. The band is beat up, pocked.

Does Marit want to hear a sob story? and she tosses back her golden shot and shakes her head hell no! And then she leans toward him, cleavage opening, to murmur in his ear these words:

Tell me in the morning.

Dale's third or fourth shot of tequila is doing laps in his stomach as she makes her oblique suggestion and his toes are curled on the edge as they would the bumpy lip of a diving board—which is where he is, obviously, right here.

One thing Dale has learned in his life is that women appear to be impressed by four star hotels, and El Paso has a fine one just down the street, quite possibly within walking distance.

I found a book in the desert: a paperback called *World War III*. I'm not kidding, by——. Open and weathered brittle by the rain, wind, sun. I leafed through it and brushed sand from its pages and it was still readable with effort, copyright 1983, rippled, beaten, hard as the shell of a yucca flower, pages the color of mesquite thorns, white stained tobacco brown, water stains the shapes of desert horizons, the layers of desert sunsets, pages pressed into the terrain of weathered sand dunes, the mesquite berms. Yellow sand, tan sand, pink, pearl, flesh-toned. Abandoned pebbles, formations like birds, formulae in the dry washes.

And I thought it seemed fair that she wanted to be on top. It seems to me that women have been the aggressors all my life, that it was the girl who wanted to take me for a ride. In fact, it was Anna who picked me up when we met, asking me if I surfed, telling me I looked to her like a surfer when I had never touched a surf board in my life. It was Marit who paid for the room, she who supplied the condoms and the heat, the urgency in her mouth.

But I couldn't perform, despite all the coaxing or whatever she tried to convince me. We ended up passing out entwined in each other, like fingers, wrapped tightly. Maybe that meant more to her, because I woke to find her watching me sleep, and she was stroking my forehead.

I'm married, too, she said when I was awake.

"I'm not anymore," I said. She nodded. Marit's lustrous hair lay over her shoulders and breasts and tendrils of it lay on my throat. I felt desire then, but it was only to feel good and I didn't think anything in the room could make me feel better. She might have been drawn to that in the start, whatever expression my face held when I first walked into the club and she chose me, just like men say they are drawn to sadness in women, with the feeling or desire to help them, to save them, to save themselves. I am the poster child of our role-reversed time.

One thing Anna said was that I never fought for her. She was always fighting me to get me back.

"Why are you here then?" I said.

Marit sighed. We were naked here and I didn't know her last name. I didn't know her favorite color, her preference in music. I knew she like dancing and apparently felt the need to get her rocks off. Too bad she found me.

But she didn't seem dissatisfied with where she was; she did not answer. She lay on her side smoothing my hair back from my temple and I was something I couldn't see to her. The way a woman is to a man—the ideal, the virgin, the whore—but women have different demands. Desires I didn't understand.

I'm here because I want to be, she answered finally. Does anything else matter?

I supposed not.

That's not what I said you said you wouldn't do it anymore well I messed up why do you keep messing up I don't know you know no I don't know are you trying to push me away I'm not trying to do anything to you you're never trying to do anything to me what's that supposed to mean I'm always fighting you to get you to come back to me I don't understand yes you do you're never the first one to come to me you're never the first one to apologize it's always me and I'm so tired of it I'm so tired of it I do too apologize first I have too said I was sorry first you don't and if you do it's only to find some way to twist it around and make it all my fault I never said it was all your fault you want me to be the one who always feels bad and I'm not going to do it anymore I can't take feeling this way anymore I'm sorry I'm such a horrible person I never said you were a horrible person that is obviously what you're saying if I make you feel this way what good am I to you I'm not supposed to make you feel this way I'm not in your life to make you unhappy you don't always make me unhappy I'm not doing you any good you know that's not true what good am I to you oh please don't ask me that you know all the ways you're good for me but I'm always making you feel bad we keep having this same argument over and over and I don't know when it's going to stop how can I make you happy what can I do I need to be able to trust you and honestly I don't know if I can you can trust me because these same things keep happening over and over again and I need you to tell me I need you to be honest with me what am I going to do what could you do that would be so bad that I would go I know you would never do anything like that but it's all these little things and they add up and after so many how can I believe anything you say you have no reason to believe anything I say you're right a sunset like a rose explosion on the edge of the sky, like ripples on a turquoise pond burst by a tossed stone, like pink skid marks into the horizon. I smear it with whiskey.

 I feel like the desert inside. I feel like the sand in the wind. I feel like the April wind that never stops and blows us away—our words, our intentions, our gestures and our life together slipping. I'm afraid of how fragile all this really is when it had seemed once like my only solid thing, my only true anchor in life. Like a ship without a rudder. Like a book in the desert. Like the plastic bag blown so far from anywhere caught on mesquite thorns and slowly shredding away tattering gradually. My stained flag. The fact is we are only what we try to be and why do I not feel like trying anymore when so many parts of me are screaming get up go on get up keep fighting, but instead I just lie here. I used to never feel like not trying or fighting for you and how have I changed. What happened to me. Where have I come to. There is no one here with me. No one where you were to pick me up. No one near me, Anna. No one where I need you to be when I reach, if I would reach. What's wrong with me. When did I start to doubt.

Well maybe we made a mistake what do you mean we made a mistake maybe you and me maybe all this maybe we did the wrong thing maybe that's why all the same crap keeps coming up and won't go away how can you say that is that what you think I don't know what I think but this same stuff keeps happening and it hasn't stopped it's been four years and it hasn't been any different and honestly I don't know if I can change I can't seem to I keep doing the same things over and over and I keep hurting you and I don't want to hurt you any more how could you say that how could you call us a mistake why do you say things like that and yes it hurts me but I just want you to stop I don't want to give up I don't want to give up either then why do you say things like that please don't push me away please don't say things like that.

Where is your wife, she asks him. He looks up into her face. She has the slight shadow of a mustache across her upper lip, but it is barely visible against her skin. Her eyelashes are still black and full, thick with last night's mascara. She moves closer to him so that her breasts rest on his shoulder. How strange the shapes and lines of her body, he thinks, the color of her skin on her flank and along her stomach. Her skin a product of a life he does not know. Her lips a movement he does not understand. The way her hair falls and her cheeks dimple are unknown to him. Her unfamiliar knees.

And a feeling of nausea passes through him that that makes him shudder—but inwardly, and he feels sick and sorry and helpless on the bed beside her. Her eyes lay on him, calm and waiting, and he can't read anything in her brown irises. He swallows. He tastes his mouth knowing something of what he tastes is her—her lips and skin and the eery warm tequila still haunting him.

The knowledge that he has hurt Anna pervades him. He feels it in his ankles. He feels it everywhere this woman Marit touches him, where her body lies warm up against him. He breathes, feeling hot and like a vacuum.

"My wife is," he says. He flexes his neck, feeling her soft fingertips on his forehead. She runs one finger down the bridge of his nose, traces his lips, then touches the finger to her own lips and places it on his lips again. Her finger is moist. She is knowing and soothing. He feels invaded by her. But he does not move.

Again: Anna wanted to leave and he let her. This is the easy answer. But he pushed her away and he didn't know if she still love him but he wanted now for her to still feel that way and love him, need him, like he needed her. Even though he had been aware, the entire process, of how he was slowly closing her out, resenting her and hating her and needing her and loving her and unable to release the clot he held inside. If the love died then it died, if he knew it for what it was, if he ever had: this love, this desire, this calling for her that was making him physically sick right now with this woman mothering him and asking after his wife when she was a wife herself and how then could she be trusted? Mustn't she hate him for his crimes, envisioning her own husband in bed with another woman who had picked him up in some dance club and taken him to a hotel and tried to arouse him but failed and instead just usurped the space and heat of his body in a hotel room bed—even a four star hotel like this one?

So to finish like this: "My wife and I separated." Right. Spit it out.

"We lost our son eight months ago and I guess we didn't recover. She flew back to San Diego last night."

Marit nods. "I'm sorry," she says. Her eyes are black and blank. "You need to relax. You're so tight. You need to calm down." Her fingers are painting his chest, his arms. Her voice is a soothing infestation. "Listen, you're heart is racing."

She lays her ear on his chest and her hair is so soft and warm.

Oh.

The sun on the white window sill, white curtains breathing. A thousand other hotel windows visible and secret on the facing wing.

Two people in a car resenting each other. A woman and man. Driving saying nothing. Fighting silently. But what joy this is to be alive and to feel. Who else would give this to me but her? Who else would make my life this way—give me these vibrant colors and this jagged experience she gives me, scenery flowing by in counterpoint to our quiet in here. She looking out the window. Her bags are in the trunk. She sighs, her hands folded in her lap. The line of her turned face against the glow of the window, warm, light-filled, suffused and faded—fading into the passing blur beyond her. A diamond earring and her hair pulled back in a pony tail away from her neck long and fine. I am in the process of losing her. I am in fixed final stages counting down mileage markers each closer to the airport freeway exit and the airport expressway and short term parking and the terminal, the check-in, the security gate metal detector, the boarding gate, the final call and then myself alone watching her back in the crowd being covered and taken.

The inane radio and the sound of the engine humming.

Before the war. Deep in the blankets her hair is a soft mess on her head—is there anything lovelier than the expanse of a woman's back as she lies in bed, arms crossed beneath her cheek. I've watched her breathe. I've traced her back from the hollow above her buttocks to the ripples across her shoulders to the long curve of her neck and the hairs on the back of her neck. Every hair is a nerve ending, a direct connection with the brain, lightly, lightly, she will murmur and bury her head deeper in sleep. There is a haze on the surface of her skin, there is a glow, a diffused essence of her in a glow surrounding her. This is how I see her. Nothing in life is like her. What is more important than right now—how could anything mean more than this and why should I have to leave her? I hate the army right now. I have to leave. I have to go from her and I don't know when I will see her again. Lying here. Lying here. What in life is more than this. What is beyond this. This moment, this morning, the sunrise light trimming the window shades pink on blue-black. She sighs in her sleep. She snores slightly. She settles deeper in her arms. Her skin is gold. Her skin is warm caramel.

Don't wake. Don't wake, Anna.

Why do people choose each other and how is this resolved? How do we fit our lives together—how do we love each other and walk side by side no one leading no one in charge? Birds fly circles around one another, ballet in the branches, orbits within orbits attracting closer, males warbling and searching, reaching in song. They have so much to say—what are they saying to each other? Come to me. Look at me. Love me. Do we run out of words to say? Do we add up history until these carefree words are just—impossible? Useless. How empty are words after these events. What can words build between us, we who held our dead creation and could not hold each other anymore. What will we make with words now—here, right now in this car traveling down this very road a woman and man, a husband and wife. Where did our bridge crumble and where did its pieces fall? How can I touch you with words? What can I attempt? I am not the drug to erase your memory. I cannot ease the soreness between your legs. I cannot take the milk from your breasts. Words won't fix these things in this car right now. What will you say to remove the image I have of you taking your wedding ring from your finger, holding to the light so its diamond flashed, and calling it a joke—will you take that from me? Will you take the tragedy of us from me, please, Anna? Will you say words that make me into the fool I was before I loved you and before I tasted life and before I loved. Will you do this for me, please, before you go? I can't say these words. I can't shape my mouth. I can't move my eyes to look on you and say these things. Who am I to love you? Who am I to need you so desperately and love you with all my being even as I watch you pack your bag so slowly, carefully and stoically with me watching, loving this new facet of you, loving your disdain for me and the dust of our love, that bridge once between you and I, now buried, now a long silent car ride home from the hospital where we said nothing to one another, nothing, knowing we had died. This—the birds sing.

Are there birds outside this hotel room? Are there birds in this desert like there were back home? I remember waking to birds in the sunlight between tree branches outside my bedroom window. Robins and jays, sparrows. Sometimes crows, black in the branches. Hold me, Anna. Touch me, please. Don't turn from me—Anna. Anna, my everything. Anna, my desire. The words I have written you—the letters I wrote to you from the desert. Those were the best of me. Words that meant something. Words that sang once. And now I feel so silent. I feel so blank without you to write on me. When I thought I might die out there in the desert away from you—when all that mattered were the words I put on paper for you. The essence of me. The progress of my pen mapping myself out for you, mapping these emotions I had then, when I wasn't afraid of what was between you and me, when everything you and I made together was the wonder of my life—the sum of me. Invested in you. Where is that paper now? I was so eager to fill it up with everything that was never enough to say to you—words against the falling missiles, words with the rising missiles, my death in the desert, drowning me with every breath. My definition for you. My beautiful wife. I married better than I deserved.

Do you remember Colonel Cabe saying that as a toast to his wife at that first Christmas party before the Gulf? It is my truth.

Dressed now. My clothes smelled like cigarette smoke and two perfumes: Anna's and Marit's. She was smoking near the window, holding the cigarette to her lips a long time, one hand holding her elbow, before she exhaled gray smoke against the morning sunlight. She was wearing my t-shirt. Did I lose it in our tangle? Her hair was white-black against the window, shot with veins of sun.
"Do you want some breakfast?" she said. "I'm buying."
Standing here with Marit, I was aware of her loneliness. This was how she found me—what brought us here. She held herself like she is unused to other arms. She was accepting of where I moved in the room, following me with her eyes. I could see her watching me in the mirror above the bureau. She was just another facet of Anna. I was here thinking of her and wondering at her reaction to this room, right now. Loving her hatred of me. The course of our relationship.
"Did you have a pet?" Marit asked.
"No. No pets."
Anna was allergic to most anything with fur. She tried with a kitten we chose from the animal shelter. It lasted only a week and she cried when we had to take the little tom back, convinced her allergy would mean his eventual death.
Marit has two dogs, she was saying. She spoke of them like her children. Her loneliness. But I wouldn't ask of her husband, the man she had chosen me over right now.
She put out the cigarette and sat on the edge of the bed and I drew her back to me, laid my hand on her chest and listened to her heart beat under her soft skin. She smelled of smoke, gray remainders still drifting near the window. She held me with one warm hand on the side of my face, sighing like she was pleased or satisfied somehow. Just to be touched.

"I can't go to breakfast," I told her. I'm going to have to be going soon. It's somewhere near eight now. I had empty hours to anticipate.

She accepted this and didn't move, her hand feeling good against my cheek. Each of these moments was separate and full lying there with her—and she was anonymous to me. She continued to talk and ask me these general questions about me but I didn't want to know her, I didn't want anything more to connect me or make her more than this sensation right now, my head on her soft breast, her hand cradling me and her body long and warm, her legs bare in the morning sun. Nothing more. Nothing else to hold me here.

The sun outside the window was bright and deep.

Escaping her, he leaves her lying on the bed watching him close the door, the narrowing entrance to her world in there until snick the door is closed and freedom fills the four star hotel hallway. A maid pushes her cart down the hall.

Dale stands looking at the door, just like every other door in the long hall, but he knows what waits behind it. He sets his head on the door and feels he is going to start crying. Is this it? Is this the bottom or somewhere near it? Will I find it?

These tears are weak. They're not real. He feels I'm nowhere near the bottom but I'm going down and why not enjoy it? Why not watch the ride? Pick yourself up before she opens the door and sucks you back in there. The freedom in the hallway is syrup sick and he feels it has to be pushed through. He has a powerful desire and need to feel the sun. He still feels as if he is in the club, bathed in the noise-silence, the world full of white noise. A flat television screen crawling with it, edged in the blue glow.

How did he pull himself free of her? The elevator is speeding down, surrounded by burnished brass and mirrors.

How did Anna leave? How did she turn her back, how did she turn her eyes from him and get lost in the crowd pressing onto the airplane.

Her perfume used to weaken his knees—now Marit's clung to him. How old did she say: 25. When he was twenty-five he had been home from the Gulf a year. They were in Fort Lewis in Washington before the move to El Paso. The year he asked Anna to marry him. When I was twenty-five—that had seemed the pivotal age to him, the proper point in that ingrained time line that listed children at year thirty. And came early: at twenty-nine but he held on inside still. Counting still.

The morning sun outside the lobby doors rejuvenates him, refreshes that smoke-stained core inside him. Smells of the street and a light breeze take all memory of the woman in the hotel room from his mind. The sky is a flat plain of dry blue, soft and borderless. The air, heat sounds: Dale feels alive suddenly, a suffusion of energy from somewhere, from his escape. He has escaped.

He thinks of how she unzipped his fly, her eyes on his. Unwrapping my present, she said.

Today is Sunday.

Sometimes—times when he was waiting for her in airports or after work—he would watch her step through a doorway and before she started to look for him, before she found him, he wondered what it would be like if they had never known each other. If her eyes moved past him rather than finding him. If he could watch her without knowing her and what would she mean to him then? Who would he be then? Discovery or loss?

He felt afraid. He felt guilty for thinking it and his punishment would be that it was true. A heartbeat of panic, a breath of cold waiting for her, needing her, seeing clearly the chasm in him if that were real, if she no longer knew or needed him. What truly makes a man afraid—when he has this to lose, all this—having known it and now that it could slip.

But her eyes—her face is cast down and then it rises and she sees him. And he feels so light.

Here we are. This is how this is supposed to happen.

Acknowledgements

The author owes a great debt to the following people for putting him in print or helping him stay there: The Elixir Crew: Mike Jones, Jennifer Johnston, Garth Marriot, Herschel Brown (Big Dog, Rio, G$, H-Bomb, repectively). Brian Dawson. Lonny Lozar. Justin Stegall. Sue + Bill. Mom + Dad. Jody Rolnick. The two people who have actually written me fan letters, thank you.

Printed in the United States
3163